D1521162

Taken by Chance
A Club Volare Novel

Chloe Cox

ISBN: 1490440224
ISBN-13: 978-1490440224

CONTENTS

A Quick Note

Just a Quick Note...

Hi you guys! Ok, I'm just going to say this up front: I love Chance. He is, of course, based on people I've known in real life (though I'm not saying more than that!), and I am a total sucker for the combination of dominating and playful. I don't know exactly why that is, but I do feel like Chance is a guy I would love to spend time with.

Ahem.

I hope you guys will love Lena, too—she's got her own issues, but she's a good person, trying to do her best, and not always succeeding. I feel for her, there. And it made me so, so happy to get these two to their own HEA.

Chapter 23 included. ;)

xoxo Chloe

Those who fly...

chapter 1

Chance Dalton counted the men gathered below the unnamed woman's apartment, pacing in circles outside her gate, sometimes yelling up at her window. Waiting with the patience of scavengers. Hunting her.

Fucking animals.

He counted to keep his mind orderly, rational. His body was already tense, his pulse providing a thick rhythm for his anger. He had to keep it rational.

He just hated men who bullied women.

There were four of them. All of them carried cameras, their stock in trade. Three of them were sweating uncomfortably in the eighty-degree heat, had guts protruding over their belts in various degrees of ill health. Chance guessed it was hard to keep in shape when your job required you to stake out celebrities for days at a time, living on fast food and candy bars, sleeping in the back of your car. The fourth was different. Skinny, wiry, jumpy, wearing a pretentious fucking blue fedora: the only one who seemed really with it. The one who kept his eye up on her window, waiting for the curtain to flick back, waiting to get a glimpse of her face.

He was the one who kept shouting up at her.

What the hell was with these people? Chance was usually the last guy to knock a paying job, considering some of the shit he'd been paid to do overseas, but this was something else. This was professional stalking. This was being paid to make someone's life miserable for a freaking photograph.

He wouldn't have noticed, probably wouldn't have given it a second thought, except this time they were after *her*.

He hadn't known she was famous, though she was certainly beautiful enough, and he definitely couldn't imagine what she'd done to merit interest from these vultures. She lived on the top floor of that modest California craftsman across the street from the walled compound that Chance had helped turn into Volare L.A. Hers was just a normal house set back from a narrow side street off Abbot Kinney Boulevard, looking peaceful and bucolic behind a high wooden fence, sun-splattered below a few shade trees. Someone had split it into a duplex sometime in the past decade — probably the gray-haired woman who lived on the first floor. The house probably sold for peanuts back in the seventies, and now it was a million-dollar house, just because Venice Beach was booming.

Somehow, even with all that dark-haired, honey-skinned beauty, *she* didn't strike him as the kind of woman who lived in a million-dollar house.

Best goddamn part of his day, every day, just watching her walk down the block to get breakfast. Always at the same time, always laughing with the older woman at her side, the two of them friends, maybe family? Always she bought breakfast for the busker on the corner, too.

Always, she had a smile for Chance.

He hadn't realized how dull his world had been until he'd gotten that smile. Sleeping around L.A. had gotten old, L.A. itself had started to feel old, and he'd had to admit that no matter where he went he was stuck with the memories of the things he'd done — and then he'd seen her.

Smiling at him. Shy at first, but so expressive. Like they had their own private joke about breakfast or coffee or whatever, even though they'd never exchanged a word. Chance had resisted the temptation to go after her the way he knew he could, had looked back on his track record in L.A. and decided he didn't want to risk that a no-strings fling with her would backfire in the way it had with so many others, leaving her bitter and disappointed. No matter how honest he was up front, women always seemed to develop feelings and want more from him, and he didn't want to see that smile disappear. But then these pricks with cameras had shown up, and now this was the second morning in a row that she hadn't left her house, and the smile was just a fucking memory anyway.

Christ, he couldn't get her out of his head. Couldn't get the things he wanted to do to her out of his head. The memories of other women just turned to ash when he thought about her. Thought about how she'd feel under him. About what she'd sound like.

He didn't even know her name.

They had her trapped up there, like an animal. Laughing together, making jokes. Like it was funny.

Just thinking about it made him angry all over again. He ground his teeth and decided the bullshit stopped here. This was his goddamn neighborhood now, his city, and that woman across the street was something special. He wouldn't ask anything of her, and he wasn't going to take advantage of her, the way he knew he could, but he sure as hell wasn't going to let these idiots hurt her, either.

"Hey." Chance heard the fedora call out. The skinny, hat-wearing pap lifted his camera to his face and Chance followed his line of sight.

Her window, the curtain held back. Just a sliver of her face flashing in the light.

She looked frightened.

Chance felt the familiar lurch in his gut, the fire crawling up his spine, down his arms, looking for a way out. What he really wanted to do—what every synapse in the primitive part of his caveman brain was telling him to do—was to go kick some ass. Show that skinny asshole what it felt like to be hunted. Cornered.

"Heel, Chance," he seethed to himself.

He was right. A minute later, he saw the door to the craftsman open. From his vantage point on one of the decks on the second floor of Volare L.A., he could see the shock of silvery hair: the older woman.

Alone.

In a minute Chance was down the stairs and running across the path to the back door. He burst through onto the street just in time to see the older woman swat at the skinny asshole in the hat and drive all the paps back from the gate.

She was kind of a badass. And older, but not

old; up close, she was one of those women who aged flawlessly, better looking than most women half her age.

Still, maybe she wouldn't mind an escort.

"Ma'am?" Chance said as he jogged up alongside her, careful to get between her and the asshole in the hat. He gave all four of them a once over. "Can I help with anything?"

She gave him a frankly appraising look, the kind of thing that might have made him blush if he'd possessed the capacity for it. Then she smiled.

"I'm just fine, but you might wait around while I go to get my breakfast to make sure these idiots don't do something stupid, like trespass on my property, or violate the privacy of my tenant."

Chance grinned for the first time all morning. "I'd be happy to, ma'am."

"Call me Thea." She winced. "I'm not that old."

"All right, Thea," he said. "Nice to meet one of the neighbors finally. Don't you want to know my name?"

"Chance Dalton, I'm very aware of who you are, and of what you've brought into my neighborhood," the woman called Thea said, a little too gleefully. "And let me tell you, I approve."

Chance laughed. "Well, all right, then. Good to know I'm welcome."

"Don't you want to know why these monsters are bothering Lena?"

Lena. So that was her name. It sounded good.

"Honestly, Thea, it doesn't seem like any of my business. But I will be happy to remove them for her."

Thea raised an eyebrow. "You know she hasn't left the house in two days? Just crying all the damn time. If I were younger I'd kick his ass myself." Thea glared at the man in the hat, who kept his eyes on the window.

Chance balled his hands into fists, opening and closing them like he was pumping a safety valve. He didn't need any encouragement to want to get physical with these assholes. "You mean that photographer?" he asked.

"Yeah, him, too," Thea sighed. Something in her tone made Chance look back at her—for a moment she seemed so sad, the kind of expression he'd seen on a mother's face when her child got hurt.

That didn't help.

"I'll only be a few minutes," Thea said, walking away.

Chance barely heard her. His attention was now focused on the four men crowded around Thea's gate. He moved toward them and they moved back. He stood between them and the gate, his arms crossed to keep him from feeling the itch too bad, feeling Lena's eyes on his back as he took his post and feeling weirdly proud of it. Which was ridiculous; he didn't know her. He knew why he was doing what he was doing, and it had everything as much to do with his own baggage as it did with wanting to protect a woman he didn't properly know.

Well, so what? he thought to himself. Sometimes it just felt good to do the right thing.

The four paps backed off a few more feet, one of them cursing, heading back to a car parked down the street. Three remained, the skinny one looking right at him. What Chance *wanted* to do was smash their cameras, the weapons they used to harass a woman from a cowardly distance, see if any of them were man enough to fight. Hoping one of them was that dumb.

But Chance also knew that that was technically kind of insane. He knew that would only scare the woman watching from the window behind him, and rightly so.

"Goddamn common sense," he muttered to himself.

One of the paps looked at him with even more alarm. Chance smiled. There had to be a way that he could help Lena get out of here without committing a felony or scaring the shit out of her. No matter what the story was, no matter what she'd done—if she'd even done anything at all—she didn't deserve this. There had to be something he could do, something that would work in a place like this…

By the time Thea came back with her breakfast burritos, Chance was grinning to himself, freaking out the paps even more. Maybe he could have some fun with this. Maybe he had a plan.

~ * ~ * ~

Lena made a deal with herself: if she let herself peek through the curtain again and *he* was still there, she'd…

Nope. She couldn't think of anything. There were no household chores left to do. She'd done them all. She'd done all of Thea's, too — anything to keep her busy and inside the house. She had nothing to bargain with.

Nothing to hide behind.

Lena felt the tears coming again and cursed. She was so damn tired of crying. Of being a victim. Of letting Richie do this to her, of allowing those jerks outside to get to her. Her frustration would build until she'd almost reached her limit, where her anger at what they'd done to her would begin to outweigh the anxiety and humiliation, and she'd be on the verge of storming outside to curse them out and find her car, when she'd remember. She'd remember that Thea, who was taking care of her so kindly, who was like a best friend and a fun aunt all wrapped into one, that even Thea must have seen the photos that Richie leaked online. Thea, who read her trashy magazines religiously, had probably opened one and gotten the surprise of a lifetime.

So she'd remember that Thea had most likely seen those pictures, and then she'd remember that everyone she knew had probably seen those pictures, and the shame would come back with such intensity that it actually paralyzed her. As though if she were to stop moving, stop even breathing, she might be able to will herself to disappear, to obliterate the whole thing even from memory…

Lena didn't even feel right complaining. She'd had just enough success as an actress that people might recognize her if she jogged their memory, that people assumed she must be rich because she'd been on TV. She wasn't. And she was just hot enough and just recognizable enough that a narcissistic ex-boyfriend might decide to leak some explicit photos to rejuvenate his own career.

But Richie had done worse than that. He'd convinced her to do things she hadn't ever been brave enough to do before. He'd fucking *groomed* her. And then he'd secretly taken photos.

Lena shook her head. The worst part was that this reaction, this hiding away from it, the freaking crying? None of it felt like her. She'd always been tough as nails, hard and suspicious after a lifetime of watching people use each other, and now it was like something was broken. Maybe it was just one transgression, one disappointment too many. Maybe L.A. had just used up all she had left. She was trying not to think about it, but she was trapped in the freaking house with nothing to do, not letting herself go online, not watching TV, and with those photographers waiting outside. Hard not to be reminded pretty much constantly.

And now *he* was involved. Chance Dalton. The man who'd occupied her thoughts pretty much since he'd moved in across the street. To be fair, he'd probably occupied most people's thoughts. Six foot a million, buzzed head, wicked smile, blue eyes that sparked over dimples, military tats over arms like thick bunches of steel cable, and the man shows up in L.A. to run the sex club everyone wants to join. So, on top of all that, obviously he must be amazing in bed.

Practically all of female L.A. had thrown themselves at him. And they kept throwing themselves at him, because the rumors were that he *was* amazing. If you believed those same rumors, he'd already done half the women in L.A., and they'd line up to give him seconds. Everybody wanted him. Hell, they probably would have been after him even if he'd been a nobody—just looking at him was enough to get Lena wet. It was nothing short of a miracle that any man could interest her in that way after what Richie had done, but Chance was definitely not just any man. The black t-shirts and jeans did nothing to hide the musculature underneath, or the smooth, athletic grace of the way he moved, like he just enjoyed using his body. Using bodies. Everything about him seemed just one step removed from the wild.

And every time he looked at her, she felt naked.

Just, something in his eyes, even from across the street…

Much better to be thinking about him. Lena flicked aside the curtain and stole another look outside. He was still there. With his arms crossed, staring at the photographers, who were now huddled together across the street. Were there fewer of them now?

Wait, what the hell was going on? He looked like he was guarding her house. A man she'd never had the guts to talk to, who she was sure had barely noticed her amidst all the incredibly beautiful women who threw themselves at him all day long, looked like he was standing guard over her.

Lena shook her head. That was *ridiculous*. Maybe not any more ridiculous than her actual life at the moment, but ridiculous nonetheless.

She was probably just getting cabin fever. Or it was wishful thinking. Or…

"Thea?" Lena whispered.

Her landlord-turned-adopted-family had just come down the street, carrying a take-out bag from the breakfast burrito place and smiling. Smiling? And…stopping to talk to Chance?

"Oh shit," Lena said quietly. "Oh shit, oh shit, oh shit."

Thea was nothing if not impulsive. And nosy. And meddlesome. And impish. And possibly Lena's favorite person on the planet, but that didn't keep Lena from experiencing a wave of panic when she realized that Thea had turned all of those talents on Chance Dalton.

Chance Dalton, who remained the one guy she could fantasize about safely. Thea was…

Oh God, they were laughing. Together. Like they were planning something. Chance turned around, looked right at her, and waved. Then he held up one finger, as if to say, 'just one minute,' winked, and jogged back across the street to disappear into the Volare compound.

Lena jumped back from the window, eyes wide open, blinking fast. What the hell did that mean? What? How long had he been out there? Oh God, had he been talking to the photographers? What if that wink…

Another horrible thought struck her: he must know, too. Just like Thea. He must have seen the photos. And the paparazzo scum outside her house would know who he was, just like she did. They'd know he ran Volare, they'd know Volare's reputation. Lena was momentarily overwhelmed by horrifying visions of the paps bringing Chance into the story, asking him lewd questions, making ridiculous insinuations, as though Lena hadn't already been humiliated enough. The thought of Chance playing along with that…

She shook her head. *Stop being crazy*, she told herself. *You don't know him and he doesn't know you. Besides, would it be so much worse for one more person to have seen those photos?*

But somehow it did feel worse. Lena had kept herself cooped up in her apartment, hidden away from reality, to protect herself from all this crap, and she'd let her imagination run wild to comfort herself. She didn't realize what a big part Chance Dalton, a man she didn't actually know at all, had played in those escapist fantasies until now. So what if it was a little foolish, and maybe adolescent, and kind of weird? It had worked. It had given her a break from remembering that the last man she had trusted, despite all of her experience, despite everything she'd seen in this industry, had ruined her career by violating her privacy so completely that the idea of trusting anyone ever again now seemed hopeless naïve.

Well, that tiny little comfort was gone now. If Chance hadn't seen the pictures yet, he was probably looking at them right now. Back to cold, hard reality.

"Lena?"

Lena turned around to see Thea setting down the food on the coffee table. Lena couldn't help but envy the incredible shape her friend was in—she'd never guess the woman was nearly seventy if she didn't know it from being Thea's emergency contact. Lena figured it had to do with a positive outlook and enjoying life, something that normally rubbed off on her. But now that they were in private, Thea didn't bother to hide her worry.

"Honey, are you *trying* to become the neighborhood cat lady shut-in?"

"Um…" Lena looked around. She hadn't turned on the overhead light and the sun had passed mostly overhead while the curtains were still drawn, so she was, technically, sitting kind of in the dark. By the window. Crouched behind the closed curtains. "Not on purpose," she said.

"This is too much, Lena. You have got to get out of here, have some fun, get your mind off things. At this rate by the time you step out into the sun you're going to burst into flames like a damn vampire."

Lena snapped her fingers. "You still have my *Buffy* DVDs! I've been looking for those."

"I'm serious."

"I know," Lena said. She could feel the heavy weight in her chest start to twist again, tightening around her ribcage, making it hard to breathe. She was not in a good place.

"You know it's not good for you to get out there. Avoidance is never good."

"I just can't go through that yet," Lena said softly. "As soon as I step out there, it'll just…all over again. What he did. All those questions, all the stuff they'll say about me. Remembering how he used me. I just…can't."

Thea came over to join her on the window seat and took Lena's hand gently in her own.

"Then you're going to kill me," Thea said.

Lena slowly turned her head to stare at Thea in horror. "Oh my God, what did you do? What did you say to Chance Dalton?"

"Oh, you mean that gentleman across the street whom you eyefuck every morning?"

"Thea!"

"Oh come off it, I know you're not a prude," Thea said, suddenly serious. Lena flinched at the word 'prude,' and that didn't escape Thea's notice, either. "And I *know* you're not going to let that scumbag Richie determine how you feel about yourself or your sexuality. Right?"

Lena closed her eyes. Sometimes she'd prefer to have a best friend who was somewhat oblivious. Thea had a tendency to see straight to the heart of an issue and head right for it, preferring to be blunt over tactful. She used to say that the older you got, the less inclined you were to waste time dancing around the stuff that mattered, but Lena had a suspicion that she'd always been like this.

Lena didn't feel quite ready for it at the moment.

"Please just tell me what you did."

"First, I only did it because I care about you."

"Stipulated. Go on."

"And second, I don't know exactly what I did."

"Thea..."

Thea shrugged. "Well, he was very eager to help. He seemed genuinely offended by this whole situation, which I think speaks to his character, does it not?"

Lena groaned. "Offended by the situation" could mean many different things. It could mean that he'd check out the story and decide she was just a cheap whore, just like everyone else, or worse, that she leaked the story herself for publicity.

Which, in this town, wasn't a crazy assumption. But it also wasn't Lena. Maybe she'd never been a good fit for this place. Or for this career.

"He said he had an idea to help get you out of here," Thea went on, her voice mellowing. "No idea what, though. And he gave me his phone number."

"…What?"

Thea cackled. "So I could check up on him, honey. Old fashioned, in a way. Strange for a man who runs a sex club, don't you think?"

"Honestly, Thea, I have no idea what to think about anything. I am incredibly tired of thinking. I just…oh crap."

Lena was peeking out the window again, and this time there was something new: a black vintage muscle car with a white racing stripe, a Mustang or a Challenger or something, rumbling up the narrow side street to come to a halt directly across from her window, on the far side of the street.

She also saw that the photographers were back right outside the gate, waiting. None of them bothered to turn around and look at the car that sat idling, the massive engine audible from across the street.

But Lena did. And she saw Chance Dalton get out, look right at her, and wink.

Without thinking, she waved back. And she laughed. First time in two days she really felt like laughing. The man was just…incorrigible.

And gone.

As soon as he saw her wave, he jumped back in the car and drove out of sight, and reality came crashing back down on Lena in a crushing wave. Nope, she was still stuck here, still in this situation, still with a ruined image that no one would ever take seriously again, if they ever had. Still humiliated, still violated, and with what remained of her professional dreams in ruined tatters.

Then Thea's phone rang.

"You didn't," Lena said.

Thea looked down. "Of course I did. And it is him."

"Jesus."

Lena's heart was pounding, but really, why? Why was this making her any more anxious than she'd been since the photos had been published? She was such a mess.

But Thea was already talking.

And handing over the phone.

"He wants to talk to you."

Lena felt a little queasy and her hands felt cold, the way they did when she got really upset. Her body was an absolute coward, and her mind was a little disgusted with it. Her mind, in fact, was starting to reach the limit of its patience with this whole thing. She had been in L.A. for ten years. She had thicker skin than this.

"Hello?" she said into the phone. Thea did a triumphant little fist pump.

"Hey, Lena. This is Chance. Thea tell you about me?"

"Briefly."

"Good." She could tell he was smiling, even over the phone. Confident bastard. "Lena, I've got a question for you. That gate out in front of your house—does it open outward or inward?"

Lena felt like she was hearing things. "What?"

"Outward or inward?"

Lena felt her mouth open and close, open and close, like a fish. What kind of bizarre…?

"You ok, Lena?"

"Fine," she said. She had to close her eyes and visualize the gate. "Inward. What is this about?"

"Excellent," he said. "It's about the fact that I hear you're trapped up there by a bunch of idiots with cameras, that correct?"

And now Lena felt ridiculous all over again. Silly. Childish. On the one hand, she was shattered. On the other, what a silly set of problems to have.

"Well, not physically trapped or anything," she said, feeling worse by the second.

"Don't do that," the voice over the phone said. It was gruff without even trying, amazingly male. She couldn't help but listen. "Don't belittle this bullshit. My cousin Lola was in a situation like that not too long ago. I know how bad it can be."

Lena's mind latched on to this, grateful to have anything to think about besides her own embarrassment: he meant Lola Theroux, the woman who ran the original Volare club back in New York. She'd just married the owner, Roman Casta, and it had even gotten press coverage in L.A..

Ok, maybe he did know what he was talking about.

"So Lena," that voice said, "I'm going to help you get out of there. All you have to do is say yes."

Every defense Lena had acquired in the past ten years in L.A. went on high alert. That, and she was trapped up here because of the wounds inflicted by the last man she'd trusted — a guy who turned out to be using her for something, like the rest of them.

"Why would you want to help me?" she snapped.

There was a pause, one of those silences that seemed to hold more weight than others.

"Watch your tone," he said, his voice rumbling just like that engine outside. It penetrated something deep inside her and flipped some kind of switch. She felt...different. Good. She didn't know what was happening. "And to answer your question, Lola would kill me if I didn't."

Why did she get the feeling that was the truth — but not all of it? More troubling was the fact that she just *wanted* to believe him. She knew Volare had a reputation for ruthlessly protecting the privacy of its members, and she knew Chance had dodged every opportunity for self-promotion since he'd arrived. None of that should matter. She didn't *know* him. And she'd just learned that, even with a guy you thought you knew, you could never be sure.

But something about that voice…

"Damn it," she said.

"I'm taking that as a yes," he laughed.

"Listen, Mr. Dalton—"

"Chance."

"Chance, it's a nice thought, but these guys will be gone as soon as something else interesting happens. They'll forget all about me. Really."

"Maybe," he said. "But don't you want to give them a giant middle finger first?"

Lena was struck momentarily speechless. She'd had no idea how much she wanted exactly that. Had no idea how much she wanted to break free of this whole bullshit situation, how much staying inside, trapped, broken by what Richie had done, had made her feel so much worse, like a powerless victim. Like she had no control over her own life or what happened to her. She hadn't once articulated to herself that what she really wanted to do was give them all a giant middle finger—metaphorically—until Chance Dalton showed up.

"Yes," she said. "Actually, yes. *Hell* yes."

"That's what I like to hear," he laughed. It was an amazing sound.

"What are you going to do?" she asked.

"Don't worry, it's probably legal," he said. The sound of the engine gunning came through loud and clear over the phone. "Look out your window, then come downstairs."

chapter 2

"*Probably* legal?"

But Lena was holding a dead phone. He'd already hung up, and she could hear the dull roar of the massive engine approaching in the distance.

"Anything I should worry about?" Thea asked. She looked entirely too pleased with herself.

"No idea," Lena said. She peeked out the window again with no clue what to expect. Surely the guy wasn't a maniac or anything? No. No, that was just her battle-hardened distrust of people trying to convince her to never talk to another man ever again.

Right?

The way he'd told her to watch her tone, like if he'd been here, he would have actually done something about it... The thought sent warmth flooding through her.

The photographers were gathered outside the gate again, so that if she wanted to leave, she'd have to run their gauntlet. Just Lena's luck to be a tabloid fixation during the one week of summer when nothing else was happening, and these guys had nothing better to do. All of them looked bored and annoyed, except for that skinny one. That one...that one gave her the creeps.

The sound of the car was getting closer.

A few things clicked for Lena in the remaining seconds. One, if this was a jailbreak, it implied that she would be...breaking. With Chance. Leaving with him. Getting into his car. The thought set off a scattered storm of conflicting emotions and thoughts. There, in her gut, was...excitement? And now her mind was freaking out about how stupid and insane that was, even given the laundry list of rationalizations she had at her disposal. He was well known. He'd given Thea his number.

And he'd made her laugh. This guy who she'd never met, really, going out of his way to make her laugh about a situation that just a few minutes ago had made her cry.

He made her feel like she was capable of *doing* something.

His voice had held the promise of something darker, something sterner.

Something sexual.

Holy crap, he was driving into the group of reporters.

"Thea!"

Lena yanked back the curtain so her friend could get a good look. Immediately Thea started laughing. Chance's car, only partially visible over the top of the wall in front of the house, was slowly but inexorable pushing the reporters away from the gate. It was almost gentle, which seemed to infuriate the photographers more than anything. They were *embarrassed* by how impotent they were against gentle nudges from a car, bumping against it and squawking in fury.

It was amazing.

The skinny one in the fedora slammed on the hood of the black car, right in the middle of the white racing stripe, and Chance actually stopped. There was a pause, and then the photographers all seemed to start shouting at once, as though stopping the car were an admission of weakness or defeat. Chance let them get all worked up, then kicked the car into gear and nudged some more.

She could just picture that mischievous smile.

Lena had tears of laughter on her cheeks when she figured out what he was doing. He'd driven the car up as close as possible to the wall around Thea's house, where there would be a sidewalk if the street was big enough for one, and he'd pulled up so that the passenger's side door lined up perfectly with the gate. That's why he'd asked about which the gate opened. All she had to do was go out, open the gate, and get in the car. The photographers wouldn't get close enough for a shot.

"That's kind of brilliant," she whispered.

Chance honked the horn. It was now or never.

"You going?" Thea asked.

Right then, Lena decided to stop thinking so much.

"Screw it," Lena said. She grabbed her phone, kissed Thea on the cheek, and ran down the stairs, just in case all her reservations and fears tried to catch up with her.

Lena should have known the guy in the fedora would have figured it out, too.

She ran down the short path from the front door to the gate, elated now rather than scared, and eternally grateful to Thea for putting in such a high wall around the property. As soon as she opened the gate, Chance leaned across and opened the passenger's side door.

She was just sliding in when the photographer with the fedora saw what was happening and jumped on the hood of the car, his camera aimed directly at Lena's stunned face.

Chance was out of the car almost too quickly for her to process the information. Lena saw a strong, tattooed arm reach out and grab the photographer's belt, and then the photographer was flying backwards off the hood while his flash discharged uselessly at the blue Los Angeles sky.

Lena blinked. Chance had his back to her—a very broad back, his t-shirt clinging to muscles she didn't even know existed—one hand holding up the photographer off the ground so his head didn't crack on the asphalt like a melon, the other seizing the camera.

"What the hell is wrong with you?" Chance barked.

He dropped the photographer, gave the others a fierce glare while they huddled across the street, too late to get the shot, and got back in the car.

"Christ, what an asshole," Chance muttered. He removed the memory card from the camera, put it in his pocket, and then tossed the camera to the pissed off photographer, now hatless and lying on the ground.

"You ready?" Chance said. It was the first time he'd looked directly at her, close enough to touch her.

And oh God, those eyes.

Those arms.

Those dimples.

Holy shit.

He grinned at her, that devilish, beguiling, totally disarming grin, muscles roiling underneath tats that looked almost alive while he flexed his fingers on the steering wheel, and Lena felt her heart begin to thud. She had goosebumps. Her mouth was dry.

And oh God, she was wet.

He didn't wait for an answer, but peeled off down the street, eyes smoldering.

~ * ~ * ~

Chance wasn't prepared for what she would do to him up close.

God*damn*.

The woman was smoking hot in just jeans and a white tank top, no makeup, tussled black hair pulled back from her face without any regard to appearance. She'd looked at him with those hazel eyes, laughing and grateful and looking like she had a secret, all at the same time, and he'd gotten half-hard.

Which was going to make it difficult to keep his hands to himself. He'd promised himself he wouldn't touch her. Wouldn't take advantage of a woman in an obviously distressed situation.

But Jesus, he wasn't a saint.

Far from it.

And she'd responded when he'd told her to watch how she talked to him. If she was a true sub, he didn't know if he could hold out.

"So where do you want to go, jailbird?" he said.

When she didn't answer, he looked over at her and his heart dropped to see that the joy had drained out of her face. She'd been happy, no doubt about it, and she'd obviously found the whole thing funny, just like he did, like they were on the same wavelength. And all that had an incredible affect on him: the need he'd felt to beat the crap out of those photographers had faded, replaced by...her. Just her presence.

But now she looked worried. The Dom in him wouldn't allow it.

"What's wrong?" he asked.

They were driving at a much more reasonable speed now, just cruising around Venice. He still didn't know Los Angeles too well, but he'd gotten the hang of Venice Beach and Santa Monica. Either way, he was determined to take her anywhere she wanted to go, and protect her for as long as she needed him to.

"Tell me," he ordered. "Jailbreaks don't work too well if they scare you."

She waited a little too long before she spoke. He could practically hear the gears turning in her head.

"I'm just still trying to figure out why you're helping me," she finally said. "I mean, I can think of a few possible reasons, but I don't like any of them."

He raised an eyebrow. "Can't a guy just be nice?"

"Not in my experience," she said. She was winding herself tighter by the second.

Somebody had really done a number on her. It pissed him off.

He tossed her his phone and turned the car around.

"Call Thea if you want. Call anyone in there."

"Where are we going?" she said.

"Back to Volare. We'll go in the other side. I can drive right through the gate—no one'll see you. You're welcome there as long as you want, and you can decide what you want to do," he said, keeping his voice level. Last thing he wanted to do was spook her even more.

She nodded. He hated to see the light in her eyes go out. He caught himself thinking of ways to bring it back and then shook his head, as if he could clear those thoughts away.

But by the time he pulled in through the remote controlled gate and into the covered garage, Lena looked like she was about to cry.

Damn it.

"Ok, Lena? Listen. Tell me what's wrong. This whole thing is busted if it upsets you."

She laughed, but it was bitter. "What's wrong is now I feel like an asshole," she said, wiping a tear away from her eye. "And scared. Both."

Chance laughed, too, as he walked around the car to open her door.

"Being an asshole is underrated," he said, offering her his hand. "I like to do it from time to time myself."

She smiled again, lighting up the whole garage. Felt like the best thing he'd managed to do all week.

"So this is just a brief sojourn into heroism?" she asked.

The word "heroism" hit him hard, just as she placed her warm, soft hand in his. Chance felt knocked right on his heels, standing there open-mouthed, trying to think of something true he could say that wouldn't destroy that happiness in her eyes.

He forced himself to smile. "I'm not a hero, Lena," he said. "I'm not even a particularly good guy."

She didn't look away. More to the point, she looked deep into his eyes. Like she saw right through him.

She was mesmerizing.

Suddenly he was fighting—hard—to keep his promise to himself and keep his hands off of her.

"We'll just have to disagree about that for now," she finally said.

She was too freaking much. He said, "You

are just hot and cold, huh?"

"It's part of my mystique," she said, grinning. "Besides, I can always change my mind."

"You feel safe now?"

"Safer."

"How do we get you all the way to safe?"

Neither of them had moved. He was still standing beside her door; she was still between him and the car. So close to him. The image of her, naked on the hood of his car, legs spread for him...

What a thing to be thinking about when he wanted her to feel safe. Jesus.

"I don't know," she said softly. She looked as conflicted as he was. "I've had a weird few days."

Chance wanted to hunt down whoever had hurt her and take her in his arms, all at once, and neither of those things would be good for either of them. Christ, he could smell her. She smelled like coconut and sex and something else he couldn't identify, but wanted more of immediately.

He couldn't have this conversation like this. Being this close to her was distracting, and he had to address what was bothering her first. He was beginning to think she really was a natural sub—and that she needed a Dom to help her through this moment.

"Ask me anything," he said, turning

around. He was starting to feel jumpy, his muscles twitching alive. He'd never wanted anyone this way but he was determined to do right by her. He didn't even turn to see her follow him, knowing he'd see those unbelievable breasts bouncing in a flimsy tank top. Maybe he could get her a sweatshirt or something.

"Ask you anything?" she said, hurrying behind him.

"Yup, what I said. Tit for tat. I'll answer anything you want, then I ask you. We get to know each other. You feel safe and can relax. Ok?"

He needed to get her somewhere neutral. Immediately. Somewhere where there'd be some kind of obstacle between the two of them. Somewhere he could get the information he needed to help her, quickly.

"You really don't know what the story is?" she said, grabbing his hand. He stopped and turned around to find her eyes wide and expectant, like she'd just asked him the most important question she could think of. "You really haven't seen the pictures?"

Damn. Pictures. He didn't need details. If they were at all the kinds of pictures he was thinking of, he could understand why she'd be suspicious of men who suddenly wanted to get to know her.

Obviously someone had done that *to* her.

She wasn't a fame whore; she was fucking traumatized.

"Jesus," he said. She flinched, and he struggled to figure out how to make it better. "I meant...shit, Lena, no, I haven't seen any pictures. I have no idea what happened to you, but if it messed you up this bad, it must have been terrible. I'm not going to see them, either. You tell me about when you're ready, but as far as I'm concerned, you're just the girl next door, you understand?"

They had stopped under the trellis that covered the walk from the garage to the main building, and the warm California light was falling on her face in shifting patterns, twisting and turning in the slight breeze coming in off the water. Every time he looked at her, she was more beautiful. He was twisting up inside, just trying to keep himself from thinking about how much more beautiful she'd be when she came, pissed at himself for having a dirty mind with a woman who'd already been sexually violated once this week. That was the last goddamn thing she needed.

He was determined to be the good guy this time. He'd have to be all Dom with her. See how she reacted to what was going on inside, and take it from there.

"The girl next door," she said, with a kind of sad smile. "I'll take it."

"Was that one of your questions?" he said,

unable to help himself. He wanted to see that pure smile again.

"No, you don't get off that easy."

She had to use the phrase "get off?" Chance shook his head, and it was just as ineffectual as the last time. "Wouldn't have it any other way. Look, let's at least get inside, then you can grill me all you want."

Lena looked at him. "I will."

chapter 3

Lena tried not to pry, as a general rule, but this was the new Volare club. Everyone wanted in, nobody knew would be in and who would be out, and here she was.

It was amazing. The club must have bought six lots, all contiguous, maybe more, and turned the whole thing into a walled compound. Some of the houses had been rebuilt, some had been torn down. There were landscaped gardens and water features, a pool, a hot tub—Lena's mind lingered there for a while—a spa, hammocks swinging in the trees, all of it shielded from outside view. The whole place looked absolutely blissful, and she hadn't even been inside yet.

And Chance...

The man's presence just overrode every

rational thought in her brain. It was like she kept slipping into the moment when he was around, forgetting what was going on in her life, just enjoying herself. And then with a start she'd remember, and she didn't know whether to be suspicious or embarrassed or...well, turned on.

Whenever he gave an order—and they were definitely orders—she was positively turned on.

She couldn't help it. She doubted any woman in her position would be able to keep her head straight, but she wasn't most women. She knew better than most how risky it was to trust anyone.

Yet she could feel herself looking, searching, *yearning* for a reason to trust *this* man.

Totally nuts.

"You ok?" he said again. He was holding the door open for her. She must be such a distracted mess.

"Just grand," she said, and stepped inside. *Holy...*

She had expected something serene and private. Instead they had just entered a great room that was buzzing with activity. There were dozens of people running around, clearing out furniture, setting up giant sculpture lights that looked like...sea creatures, maybe? It looked like every crazed party planning process she'd ever seen. Like a wedding, only with a lot less lace and a lot more leather.

Oh my. What was *that* contraption?

Lena looked at him. "Dude."

Chance laughed again. She loved to hear it—it was like warm gravel, somehow. She didn't even know what that meant. He was actually making her lose it.

He said, "Yeah, this stuff isn't really my thing. I'm more about the actual party."

She could imagine. *Do NOT look back at that equipment.*

"I didn't know you guys had opened, officially."

"We haven't. Tomorrow night's a special preview for special people. You wanna come?"

Lena tried to hide her reaction. Well, if she hadn't believed him before when he'd said he hadn't seen the pictures, she did now. Because if he had seen them, claimed not to, and then he'd invited her to an obviously BDSM-themed party, he would be kind of a jerk. And whatever else was going on, she had confirmation that, at the very least, Chance Dalton cared about doing the right thing.

"I don't know if that would be such a good idea," she said. "Under the circumstances."

Chance flashed those dimples again. "I think you might change your mind. And there's always an open invitation for the girl next door."

Awkward moment. Made even more awkward when Lena saw someone she actually knew from real life in the milieu: Adra, her agent's former assistant. She hadn't seen Adra in months, but had always liked her, especially in comparison to Lena's sleazebag agent, Dan. The guy kept trying to get her to "cash in" on Richie's leaked photos. He'd even wanted to know if there was a video. Lena had just stopped taking his calls, which maybe wasn't the smartest career move, but it wasn't like she had a shot at the career she wanted now, anyway.

And she really didn't want to talk about all that with someone who had probably seen her naked in the last two days.

"Chance, can we maybe go somewhere with fewer people?" she said.

The moment Lena recognized someone, the crowd of people began to press in on her. All she could think about was that they all knew. What they all thought of her. What they'd all think of seeing her here, with Chance.

And then her inner cynic thought, *Maybe that's what he wanted all along. Maybe he is just trying to drum up publicity for the club. Or maybe I'm just a fun conquest.*

She *hated* her inner cynic. But it didn't matter. Inner cynic would speak, and Lena would be unable to ignore her, because her inner cynic was almost always right. And now all the progress she'd made—getting comfortable with Chance, getting comfortable with *anyone* who wasn't Thea—seemed to evaporate.

Chance looked at her with those blue eyes, and she felt transparent.

"Yeah, come on," he said, and led her to a stairwell.

They climbed forever in the dim light of the back stairs, Lena doing her best not to watch Chance's ass in those jeans. When they finally emerged, it was on a roof deck, but not the dry, arid concrete of most Venice roof decks. Someone had landscaped this one. It was just as green and lush as the gardens downstairs, and felt just as private, with vines and flowers and even one tiny tree.

Chance walked over to the wall around the edge of the roof, most of it covered with honeysuckle, and took in the view. When he turned back to Lena, his smile was dazzling.

"This better?"

Did this man have any idea how beautiful he was? It was almost harder to look at him than it was to look directly into the sun. He stretched out his arms and threw his head back, just an animal happy to be out in the world, and oh God, there was that V right over his hips again, the bottom part of what Lena knew would be an eight pack, leading directly down...

Her inner cynic went nuts.

"What are your three biggest fears?" she blurted out.

Chance snapped his head down to pierce her with those eyes again. Lena felt her embarrassment rising from her toes up, like she was a freaking mercury thermometer measuring the level of social awkwardness. But she couldn't help it. The more she felt drawn to this man, the more vulnerable she felt, and the more vulnerable she felt, the more her defenses kicked in. She was freaked out because for some reason she wanted to please him, and she was desperate for a reason to trust him, or at least a reason to feel like she knew him, even a little bit.

Because her heart already felt like she did. And her inner cynic knew her heart was a moron.

And it was her stupid, idiot heart that was threatening to take over, her heart that was beating dangerously fast as he walked over to her with his square jaw clenched shut, his brow furrowed, his eyes worried. He stopped just short of her, and she almost willed him out loud to just touch her. There was some kind of field between them, something that pulled at her core, something that she wouldn't be able to resist for much longer.

What *was* it about him?

"Three is cheating," he said. "I'll give you

number three. Then it's your turn."

"Ok," she breathed. He was so close. She could smell him. No cologne, no spice, just...male. "You already know your third biggest fear?"

"I had some bad nights after I came back from Afghanistan. I got 'em ranked already."

Lena immediately felt horrible, but Chance didn't seem bothered. Not even a little bit. She could *feel* his eyes on her, unwavering, intense, raw. What was he thinking?

Did he feel this, too?

"I'm sorry," she whispered, looking down.

"Not your fault. It's always a little different, and half the time it doesn't make any sense, because dreams are crazy. But it's always someone I love dying, and always because of something I did. Something I screwed up."

"Oh God..."

Ask a personal question, get a personal answer. She couldn't believe he'd told her that. Like she deserved that confidence.

"Hey," Chance said, and tilted her chin up, forcing her to look at him. That voice again. Commanding. "There's nothing for you to feel bad about. And you owe me an answer."

"Yes, sir," she said, trying to make it a joke, like maybe that way he wouldn't see the effect he had on her.

Instead something flashed in Chance's eyes. Something hard, and hungry. It burned where their skin touched, and Lena wanted more of it. She wanted whatever she'd just seen. The hunger hit her like a blow to the chest, flooding her body, making her breasts swell, her nipples harden, her clit ache, and she sucked in her breath.

For a moment, he seemed lost in it, too. Then he snapped awake and took a step back.

"What's your name?" he asked. "That's my first question."

"Oh wow," Lena muttered. "I can't believe I didn't tell you my name."

"Tell me." He said it quick, rough. His tone made her clench, drove the ache even deeper, and she took a deep, calming breath.

Why had he walked away? Why did she care? She should be terrified of what this represented, of what Chance *was*, after what she'd been through with Richie. Richie had convinced her to finally explore the kinks she'd always fantasized about, and then he'd used it to hurt her. Chance was into the same things. She hadn't known if the rumors were true, but everything about him said that he was dominant in everything. She should want to run away. She *did* want to run away, in a way. But her body wanted to run right into his arms. It was only all the years of heartbreak and scar tissue that kept her still.

"Lena Simone Maddox," she said. "I use my middle name professionally, though."

"I like Lena."

She smiled weakly. "Me, too."

"Your turn, Lena."

Her mind was spinning. She felt light-headed—high, even. All she wanted was for him to come close to her again. She wanted his hands on her, she wanted his mouth on hers, she wanted him to help her stop thinking herself in circles. That's what she'd been doing the past two days, and it was killing her, and she was still afraid of taking the plunge.

"Why did you help me, really?" Lena said.

"Lena," he said, looking down at her. "Here's the truth. I don't like men who pick on women. And seeing you smile is the best part of my day. That's it. That's all of it. I don't want anything else from you, and I don't have much else to offer you."

Oh God.

The best part of his day…

…Much else?

That did it. Lena closed her eyes, hard, and when she opened them back up she knew what she wanted. She told her inner cynic to shut up and sit down, took a deep breath, and decided to take the plunge.

"Chance?" she said. And then she froze. What was she going to say? *Oh, hey, Mr. StupidlyGoodLooking, for some reason I feel like I want to just throw myself at you? Even though, like, an hour ago I was swearing off all human beings in general? And since that's obviously pretty weird, I figure the best course of action is to just explore that. See where it takes us.*

"Yes?" he said, turning to pin her with those eyes again.

So. Blue.

"Ok, really quickly, because in a minute I'm going to chicken out," she said, the words tumbling out of her faster than she thought possible. "Have you ever felt like your life was just spinning entirely out of control?"

Chance tilted his head slightly, waiting for her to explain herself. Only she had no explanation. This was, hands down, one of the weirdest days of her life, and now she was just going with it. Because if Chance had shown her one thing so far, it was that she felt better when she took control of what she wanted. And she wanted him. She didn't want to have to think about tomorrow, she didn't want to have to worry about the future, she didn't want to have to hope for forever with someone who was going to turn around and stab her in the back. She wanted one thing that was just...hers. One thing that would prove to herself that she wasn't entirely broken, that she wasn't used up, wasn't damaged.

One time with Chance Dalton.

Just one, incredible time. With Chance.

She walked up to him, shaking like a leaf. His eyes tracked her, burning bright, but he didn't move.

"I know what that feels like," he said slowly. "It can make you do crazy things."

They were so close now. There was a sheen of sweat on his collarbone, a little bit of delicious scruff on his jaw. From the corner of her eye she could see him flexing those large hands, open, closed, open, closed.

He feels it.

"I want to do something crazy," she said.

And she stood up on her toes and kissed him.

His lips were soft, and the scruff on his jaw felt wonderful. But he didn't move. There was a moment when she didn't think he would kiss her back at all, when she thought she'd been entirely wrong, and she started to pull away, humiliated, when he broke like a tide.

His hand on her wrist, like iron, twisting it behind her back, pulling her just out of reach.

"That was…impertinent," he rasped.

Suddenly his mouth took hers, and his hands were on her hips, her ass, lifting her high and wrapping her around him. He crushed her to him so every inch of her could feel his hardness, his heat. She moaned against his lips and ground her hips and in a minute they were on the ground, Chance on top of her, overwhelming her, crushing her. She felt his hard on, even through his jeans, pressing into her. Lena had never felt so close to coming so quickly. He took her hands and pinned them high above her head, holding her helpless and at his mercy, bit her bottom lip, and let his other hand roam hungrily over her body, mauling her breasts, ripping at her jeans…

"Please," she heard herself beg. *Beg*. "Please, Chance, I can't take it any longer," she said.

His hand gripped her hip and she hated her clothing, hated his clothing, hated anything between them. Her body rose up to him wherever his mouth was, all on its own, blessedly free from thinking about anything other than what he was going to feel like inside of her. She heard that gravel voice growl, felt the raw power of the man as he lifted her legs…

And then he put his forehead to hers, raked his hands down her body, and stood up.

chapter 4

"God*damn*," Chance said as he backed away from Lena's prone body.

She blinked. Confused. He was pacing in front of her, shaking his arms out like he'd been in a fight. There wasn't enough blood in her brain to figure out what had just happened, and her body still throbbed, needing a release.

"What—"

"Fuck!" He ran his hand over his head, still pacing, working something off.

She wasn't scared. Maybe she should be scared of whatever was happening to him, but she wasn't. None of it was directed at her. All of it seemed directed at the air, the sky, the universe, himself. His face was flushed, his eyes even bluer than before, his muscles flexing with so much raw strength…

"Chance," she said.

He kept pacing.

"Chance!" she yelled at him.

"What?!"

"What the *fuck* just happened??"

Lena stood up, not wanting to stay down and be even more humiliated, and when he turned to face her she couldn't help but see his erection. Through the jeans. Even bigger than she'd thought. She lost focus for a second — because holy hell, what was she supposed to do? — and it wasn't lost on her that he obviously wanted her, just as badly as she wanted him.

So what was the problem?

"Chance?" she said again.

He was breathing hard, and he started pacing again, like he didn't trust himself if he stopped for just a moment. Like a feral beast. She wanted that, exactly that — she wanted Chance in an animal way, and he was farther away now than ever.

"Lena, you don't know me. I don't have relationships. I don't stay with women for very long. I am a sexual dominant, no exceptions. And I would never forgive myself if I…"

"What are you talking about?"

He didn't answer her. Just stopped.

"You said my smile was the best part of your day," she said. "Trust me, I'm only going to smile a *lot* more if we — "

Those startling blue eyes opened and speared her.

"You'd do a hell of a lot more than smile," he said.

Oh God. And a dominant…

"Then what is the problem?"

"I wasn't kidding when I said I'm not a nice guy," he said. He rubbed one hand over his skull again, and then looked right at her, and she could see he'd made up his mind.

And it pissed her off.

"Who said I wanted nice?" she said. "Who are you to tell me what I need?"

"You'd be surprised."

Something in his tone had changed and he was looking at her differently now. Studying her. Thinking.

But Lena was humiliated, and righteous anger came to her almost as balm. It felt so much better to be pissed off at him than it did to be the woman he rejected. She just had to keep from crying.

"What the fuck ever. I'm not going to beg, and I don't need this," she said, straightening her tank top. What she did need was to get the hell out of there before Chance Dalton looked right through her again and saw that she was full of shit.

"Thanks for the assist with those photographers, Chance," she said. "Nice knowing you."

And Lena jogged down the stairs before he could see her cry.

~ * ~ * ~

Chance slammed his fists into the heavy bag one after the other, tearing into it relentlessly for the final thirty seconds of the round. The bell sounded and the sounds of men at work faded as they all took their minute rest. Except Chance. He dropped on his wrapped knuckles and pounded out chest-to-deck push-ups, each one burning a little deeper, nothing burning deep enough.

He couldn't get her out of his mind.

He couldn't burn it off no matter what he did.

That calm he felt when he'd been with her, that lifting of a burden he didn't even think about carrying anymore—Christ, that had felt good. He would have given anything to make her feel the way she'd made him feel with just a smile, and to know it wouldn't end with her crying over him, the way it always did. Instead he'd fucked it up.

And Lena was different. Special. He knew it already.

He was sure she was a sub. Which wouldn't necessarily change things—he was fine with subs who had some idea what they were doing, but a total newbie? Subs famously got attached to their trainers. That was the exact situation he was trying to avoid.

He'd been trying to do *right*. Chance had learned that lesson the hard way. Now he would do anything to help a woman in trouble, and still they ended up hurt. He knew he'd never make up for what happened to Jennie, and he knew he didn't deserve to, either. But damn, he thought he could do something. He *wanted* to do something, for Lena.

He couldn't forget the way Lena felt, either. The way she'd smelled. The feel of her skin while she writhed under his hand, her body tuned to his like nothing else he'd ever experienced. Chance could feel in his bones that she'd melt under him, that she'd yield, beautifully submissive, like a work of art.

Damn.

The bell rang out: another round. Chance shoved up from the ground, ready to go another three minutes without letting his heart rate drop, ready to pound the bag until his knuckles bled, if that's what it took to work this off. If being with her calmed him, the absence of her did the exact opposite, and he was more on edge than ever.

"Chance?"

Shit. Normally he liked training the kid, but today was not a day to be a freaking role model.

"What's up, Michael?" he said, wiping the sweat from his face with the back of his wrapped hand.

The kid was grinning from ear to ear, which was infectious no matter how hard Chance's lungs were working and no matter how much he had on his mind. He danced on his toes to keep his legs warm and ruffled the kid's hair.

"Come on, man," Michael whined, trying to smooth his hair back down.

"You shoulda ducked like I taught you. You training without me?"

"Yeah, if you talk to Billy for me," he said.

"Call him 'Uncle.'"

"Whatever. He's not gonna remember."

Chance frowned. Billy was punchy as all hell after fifteen years as a professional boxer, but he still had enough brains not to want his nephew to go the same way. He'd asked Chance to train the kid just to keep him out of trouble, but was adamantly, defiantly against any family of his getting in the ring for real, and it was Billy's gym. Only now, Michael had visions of the Golden Gloves, just like his uncle had when he was a kid.

"Don't be an asshole," Chance said, and went back to jabbing at the bag. "You know he's right."

"Whatever," Mike said again, rolling his eyes. "You have a visitor."

Chance couldn't help it. He thought of Lena.

It was dumb. There was no way she'd know where to find him, but she'd been on his mind constantly, and when he turned around...

The skinny pap. Wearing the same dumbass blue fedora as the day before.

"You gotta be kidding me," Chance said.

"Chance Dalton, we meet again." The little rat-faced bastard actually smiled at him and held out his hand.

Chance stared at it.

"Put that away."

"Ok, no problem. We weren't properly introduced yesterday. My name is Paul Cigna."

"I don't give a shit what your name is. I know what *you* are."

Paul Cigna's smile fell so fast it was obvious it had been fake. What lay behind it was cold and calculating.

"Ok, we can do it like that. You wanna tell me how long you've been fucking Simone Maddox?"

Chance cursed and took a step forward before he remembered Michael. The kid had just heard everything.

Rein it in, Chance.

"Michael, do me a favor and go help your uncle in the office."

But Michael's voice squeaked through, too excited to listen. "Are you really fucking Simone Maddox? She's that slut that was all up in those chains in *Sizzle*, right?"

"Hey!" Chance barked at Michael. "You, over here, right now."

Slut?

Chains?

Chance's mind went berserk. He felt the vein in his forehead start to throb and that familiar fire kindled deep in his chest. He held himself down with iron control for the kid's sake, and instead of picking up Paul Cigna and throwing him out the front door, he walked Michael a few steps away from the scum that had just invaded his gym.

Chance took a deep breath.

"Mike, listen to me, this is serious, ok? This guy is scum, and Simone Maddox..." Chance paused, tried to find the words. How do you explain this to a thirteen year old? A thirteen year old who'd seen the pictures Lena was so upset about?

Chance was furious with the world.

"Simone Maddox is not 'some slut.' You do *not* talk about her that way. While we're at it, don't talk about women that way, period. You sound like a fucking idiot. You understand?"

Mike opened his mouth as if to argue, and Chance cut him off with a glare. Where the hell did boys learn this stuff? He had been even worse when he was younger, and he wished there'd been someone who could have shown him how wrong he was before he'd had to find out on his own.

"*Don't* argue with me. You talk about women that way, you're like that guy back there. That guy is not worth the time of day. He's a piece of shit. Decide right fucking now if you want to be a piece of shit, too."

"No, man," Michael said. His voice had gone back to sounding like a kid's and not that of a teen playing tough. "I'm sorry, I didn't mean it. Honestly."

Chance ruffled Mike's hair again, surprised at the relief he felt from this one small victory. He couldn't believe what had come out of the kid's mouth. And now, at the back of his mind, was a growing understanding of what it had really meant for Lena to kiss him yesterday.

And what it had meant when he'd turned her away.

"Go talk to your uncle," Chance said. "We train tomorrow, right?"

"Yeah," Michael said. The smile was back, and that was good to see, too.

Chance almost didn't want to have to turn back to deal with Paul Cigna. But the man was obviously here for a reason.

He wasn't done with Lena.

Chance rolled his shoulders, tight from his rounds on the bag and itching for more, balled his fists, and advanced on Paul.

"What the *fuck* do you want?" he snarled.

The rodent was actually smiling. "You're

new in town, right? That's ok, I understand. I'm actually here doing you a favor, big guy, and you don't even know it."

"Get the hell out of my gym."

"Mr. Dalton, Simone Maddox and Richie Kerns is a story, whether you like it or not. I'm just looking for the most sympathetic angle, you get me?"

Chance had lost patience. This guy was the reason Lena was so messed up. This guy was the reason that thirteen-year-old kids called her a slut. He advanced on the little maggot with every intention of picking him up and dropping him outside the door when a flash exploded in his face.

Paul Cigna had taken his picture.

Chance shut his eyes and went rigid. He was afraid of what he might do if he allowed himself to move.

"Don't lose your temper, Mr. Dalton. Bad example for the kids. I'll leave my card up front. You call me when you want to talk about Simone Maddox."

By the time Chance trusted himself to move, Paul Cigna was long gone.

chapter 5

After the debacle with Chance, Lena had only gotten as far as the great room in the Volare compound before she realized that she didn't actually have anywhere to run *to*, given the risk of running into a fedora-wearing weirdo at her own house, which was why she was so lucky to have run into Adra again.

Adra had taken one look at Lena's face and hugged her. It was a shocking gesture of basic humanity, the kind of thing Lena had long since stopped expecting from players in the industry. But Adra turned out to be the exception—she'd gone out on her own as an agent, gotten involved with Volare on a trip to New York, and was just as amazing as Lena had always suspected she would be.

Of course she knew about the photos. And,

since she was a member of Volare, she knew all about dominants, submissives, and Chance, too. And she'd insisted that Lena come crash at her apartment in West Hollywood for the night while she figured herself out.

It turned out to be exactly what Lena needed to get her head screwed on right.

"I need to talk to Chance," Lena had said quietly. Her immediate reaction had been too emotional, and it had been because of all the baggage she had as a result of what Richie had done. But that wasn't Chance's fault. And she was determined to move forward, and not let Richie and those pictures control her life.

Adra sipped her wine and smiled. "That might help."

"I have no idea what to say. I don't even…"

"You'll figure it out. Sleep on it. And just as, like, an aside? Volare is an excellent place to learn about dominance and submission while keeping your privacy."

Somehow Adra felt like an old friend. Lena had actually managed to crack a smile. "Now you tell me."

Adra smiled right back. "So that's settled. You're coming to the preview with me."

Which was how Lena spent a mostly sleepless night on Adra's couch, tossing and turning and trying to figure out what she was going to say to Chance. Or, rather, what she even thought about…whatever it was that had happened.

What it was she that actually *wanted*, besides Chance's body.

Oh, man. Chance's body. Her thoughts kept returning to what it had felt like to have that powerful man between her legs, to have his hands on her breasts, his lips on her neck...

The way he'd look at her when she called him "sir." She'd figured it out later; that was a hint, just a hint, of what he'd be like as a Dom.

Just the memory of that made her wet. Of how he'd lifted her up and then pinned her down...

She felt like a teenager. No, she'd never been like this, even as a teenager. This was something else entirely. It was like he'd seeped into her skin, his scent lingering on her, driving her desire deeper and deeper inside of her. She'd never needed someone like this before — not physically.

So it was by the time Thea had come by to drop off some clothes and check on her, generally, Lena thought she might be ready to talk to him.

Might.

But nothing, nothing prepared her for Volare.

Lena didn't recognize the gardens at all. Adra led her from the garage to the path she'd seen just the previous day, and when she opened the door to the covered walkway, Lena's jaw just dropped.

She'd seen pictures of the Japanese festival of lights, but never…

They had woven tiny lights throughout the honeysuckle and bougainvillea, hung lantern from all the trees, set candles afloat in the water. She was reminded of nothing so much as a museum exhibit she'd been to once in New York about the deep sea, and the bioluminescent creatures that lived there.

It was like being on the bottom of a brilliant ocean.

"Come on," Adra beckoned. "He'll be inside."

For the first time in a *long* time, Lena was nervous. Legitimately, nauseatingly nervous. Like the kind of stage fright she used to get back in high school. She was painfully conscious of the overtly sexual nature of the place, and what her appearance would imply about those photos. That she'd been ok with him taking pictures? That she'd leaked them herself?

On the other hand, she was tired of being a coward.

Adra gave her an encouraging smile. "Chin up, Maddox. You're gonna be fine. Volare people are different, I promise."

"Let's go," Lena said.

Lena didn't think her jaw could drop any

more than it had outside. She was totally wrong.

The great room that had been such a mess of chaos the day before was now a glittering mass of just...everyone. So many people! So little clothing! And that sculpted light thing that she'd thought was a chandelier was definitely suspended high in the air above the crowd, but there were also people in it.

People who were enjoying themselves.

"Is that a sex swing?"

Adra looked up and laughed. "Uh, no, not technically. It's more of like a carriage? But they do seem to be...into it."

Lena felt a little silly for her nervousness. This clearly wasn't a judgmental place.

"Is it always like this?"

"Oh, God, no. This is kind of a special night. Normally there will be, like, theme nights, classes, private rooms—once it gets started, anyway."

Lena had about a million questions about how Volare worked, about what kind of community was involved, about privacy, about all of it, and she would have grilled Adra right there, except that she had her eye out.

And she saw Chance.

She'd heard of the whole room stopping thing before, but she'd never quite believed that it was an actual thing. For her, when she saw him standing in the middle of a group of people that were hanging on his every word, wearing just a jacket with the sleeves rolled up and a pair of jeans, exposing a broad, muscled chest and that delicious eight pack, his abs flexing with every word that passed over those luscious lips…

It was more like everything else got very quiet and very dull. Lena was aware of it all, but nothing was quite as bright as Chance Dalton holding court.

He hadn't seen her yet, and Lena was glad of the opportunity to observe him like this. She liked watching him with other people. As an actress, she'd considered it part of her craft to learn body language, to be able to read expressions, to get really good at all the nonverbal forms of communication. And what she could see in Chance, she now realized, was so terrifically rare: he gave people his whole attention. He wasn't just waiting for his turn to speak, or showing off. Every time he talked to someone, he actually listened, and he blew them away. He was always the lead. He was always, always in control.

No wonder they all wanted a piece of him. He was surrounded by women all trying to catch his eye, which Lena could understand, but it wasn't just the women. Even the men seemed to want his attention, or approval, or…something. She even recognized a few them. One of them, Roddy Nichols, was a producer who'd told her nobody wanted to read a script written by a "dumb piece of ass" like her.

Well, fair enough. Roddy was an ass himself, but he wasn't wrong about the business.

She couldn't be angry at Roddy, or even irritated at the memory of that humiliating putdown, though. She was drunk on watching Chance.

And then he saw her.

Now everything stopped. Even Chance. His blue eyes locked on her and held her in place, and Lena would have sworn that she couldn't breathe until someone blocked her view.

Someone she knew.

Richie.

"Holy shit, Lena, how'd you swing an invite? Roddy got me in, but you've been hanging so low, I didn't think you'd, uh, have the stones to come to something like this, or I woulda asked. If you'll pardon the expression."

He was grinning at her. Like he thought he was charming. Like he thought anything about what he'd just said was ok.

She felt sick.

"Hey, listen, Lena, about those photos..." And now Richie leaned in, his expression sympathetic and concerned, like she didn't know him well enough to know how good of a liar he was. Like she would ever believe anything he said ever again. Like he hadn't noticed her horrified expression, and like he would have cared if he had.

"Lena, seriously, I am so sorry. I honestly don't even know how it happened, but I figured, you know, what's done is done, right? I might as well take advantage of it, right? Strike while the iron is hot—"

"You fucking *asshole!*" she hissed. When was this guy going to stop messing with her life? When was she ever going to be rid of him? "I'm not stupid. I know you leaked those photos. I never even gave you permission to *take* them, you sick, twisted—"

"Hey, Lena, come on," Richie said, taking a step back, holding his hands up defensively. Like *she* was the bad guy. "I'm just trying to make the best of it. That's how I got the part in Roddy's new project. It's a drug addict trying to get his kids back! You think I ever would have gotten that if everyone still thought of me as Richie Kerns, child star? Come on."

"Are you seriously justifying this to me?"

"Whatever. I'm saying you should take a page from my playbook. Seize the day and all that. Go out and get some auditions or something," Richie said with a sneer.

How? How had she dated this morally bankrupt pretty boy for a *year*? The very worst part about realizing that Richie wasn't a good guy with some problems, but was instead a bad guy with some charm, was that it made her think about how lonely she must have been to fall for his act. He had always been using her, and she'd bought it because she wanted to. Now that he was done, Richie wasn't even looking at her. Lena didn't think he could see her, could see the damage he had done to her, if he tried.

This was the guy who had ruined her career. She wouldn't let him ruin her life.

"Lena, are you all right?"

Warm gravel. There wasn't a better sound in the universe. She turned, even though she knew what she would see. Chance was standing by her side, his blue eyes softened for her, his hand on her arm. Without making a big deal of it he pivoted to put himself between her and Richie.

"Is everything ok?" he asked her again.

Lena was momentarily...not herself. Richie had knocked her off balance, and she wasn't prepared for Chance, or Chance's body. She was thrown by his scent, his closeness, the mile of exposed chest in front of her. Thrown enough that she had only a moment to dread what happened next.

"Hey, you're Chance Dalton, right?" Richie said. "I'm Richie Kerns. This is a great—"

Lena saw the anger flash on Chance's face as he turned, followed by the spark of recognition as he looked at Richie. People usually did that. No one could ever figure out where they'd seen him before; it used to drive Richie crazy, being a "former child star."

But the worst part, in that split second, was figuring out that Chance knew about her and Richie. Which means he must have known about those photos. About what she was doing in the photos. About what Richie was doing to her.

Lena thought she had become thoroughly, exhaustingly acquainted with anger and shame in the past few days. But nope. This topped it. Thinking about Chance seeing her like that, knowing that she had been used?

So much worse.

"Mr. Kerns," Chance said, once more making sure he placed himself between her and Richie. His voice was still gravel, but it was anything but warm. "You are about to be escorted off the premises. If I ever see you here again, I won't tell security. I'll deal with it myself. And I swear to God, if you say one more word, I'll take your goddamn head off right now."

Lena *almost* wished she could see Richie's face through the enormous wall of Chance that was blocking her view. Almost.

Instead she looked around and saw that, despite Chance's best efforts, they were making a bit of a scene. Two giant security guys walked a petulant Richie out of the room, and she wished, desperately, that there wasn't a hush. That everyone would just start talking again, and she could go back to pretending that everyone didn't know about her and Richie and what had just happened.

Instead Chance turned around and did his best to guard her with his huge body. It was, without words, one of the sweetest things anyone had done for her in recent memory. The only thing sweeter had been when he'd rescued her in his car.

"Lena," he said.

"Chance, I am so, so embarrassed, I can't—"

"No," he said, and put one finger on her lips. Startled, she looked up and saw that same fierceness in his eyes. "That will never, ever happen again. This place will be safe for you, even if I have to vet the list myself from now on."

"You don't have to do that," she whispered. "It's your club, I'm just—"

"I'm glad you came," he said.

Lena's mouth went dry. He had his arms almost wrapped around her, his hands right at her waist, drawing her abs up tight with just the sensation of his touch, and his head was bowed toward hers with those eyes…

They were the dominant eyes.

A shiver went through her.

"Chance, I came here because there's

something I need to ask you," she choked out. When had talking become so difficult?

He didn't answer at first. He was looking intently at her face, her neck, her breasts. She saw his already impressive chest expand with a deep breath and his jaw harden.

"Good. There's something I wanted to say to you, too. How about a do-over on the roof deck?"

Without thinking, Lena bit her lip.

A do-over? Of which part?

chapter 6

For the second time in two days, Chance led the most beautiful woman he'd ever seen up to his favorite place. Only this time, he was going to make damn sure she felt better for it.

Richie fucking Kerns, in *his* club. That she had to see him here, of all places. He'd been right on the edge of losing it and Lena had brought him back. Again. Without even knowing it.

Just by touching him. By being nearby. By looking at him and seeing right through him, and calling out what was best in him: his dominance.

He thought he might have figured out how that worked. She drew him like a magnet, just focused his attention, everything he had. There wasn't anything left for idiots like Richie

Kerns, and instead he was filled with…

Whatever this was.

Holy fuck he wanted her. He could *smell* her. It was driving him insane.

But first he had to explain why he'd turned her away. He had to do what he could to take that hurt away, because he was damned if he was going to make things worse for her.

He'd figure it out.

He just had to remember to think with the right head.

And that got a whole lot harder when Lena walked out onto the roof garden in that tight, white dress with her honey skin, surrounded by thousands of golden lights, all of them showing him exactly how beautiful she was.

"Oh my God," she said, spinning around. "This is incredible."

"Yup," he said. He couldn't take his eyes off of her. Fuck the roof garden.

"Are you sure this is private?" she asked.

Chance felt his cock jump awake at that. He forced himself to look away, and it almost hurt. "Yeah, this is actually mine. Entrance to my suite is on the other end, around the corner. This," he said, pointing back the way they'd come, "is a common entrance I had put in for convenience. No one will come up here without my permission, but I can lock it if you want."

"No, that's ok."

"C'mere," he said, and led her over to a grassy area with some plush couches. He thought she might want to sit down after walking around in those heels, but instead she laughed, kicked them off, and headed right for the grass.

"Oh, this is amazing," she said, walking all over the grass in her bare feet. "I can't remember the last time I got to do this."

"You can come up here anytime you want."

She stopped squishing her toes in the fresh grass and looked at him. There. Right there. That just finished him. How did she do that? Look at him like she knew what he was really thinking? Like she knew what her body was asking for?

"You're sure you're not really a nice guy?"

"I thought you didn't want nice."

"I don't."

He was losing his focus already, just losing himself in that face. Her skin almost seemed to glow, and her eyes were soft and pure sex. Her dress, God, her dress should be illegal. Pure white, white enough to make him think he could see more, and hugging every one of those amazing curves.

If he didn't do it now, he wasn't going to last much longer.

"Lena, about yesterday—"

"No, shut up," she said very quickly, walking up to where he stood. Chance was so startled by being told to shut up that he actually did it for a second.

If she wasn't careful, she was going to earn a spanking anyway.

"What did I tell you about your tone?" he said.

She stifled a smile. "I'm sorry, honestly. Please, please let me go first," she said. "Otherwise I'll never be able to do it. There's something...oh man, this is harder than I thought. This is gonna be messy."

But it was the look on her face — open and vulnerable — that convinced him to keep quiet.

Every male instinct was screaming at him that he had this beautiful woman in front of him that he wanted more than anything else he could name at this particular moment in time, and he had to fight it every second she was standing in front of him, being beautiful, and now she was telling him he had to wait a little longer before he could explain.

God. Damn.

For her, he could do it.

"I can do messy."

She smiled. He felt good. It never got old.

"Ok," she said, taking a deep breath. "This thing with Richie, the photos? It's not just embarrassing. It's not just... It's taken so much from me, Chance. I mean, yeah, I feel pretty violated, and that has messed me up pretty good. But it's ruined my career, too."

"How?"

"Do you remember me from anything?"

She had a point. "No."

"Yeah. All of my on-screen roles have been, like, Slutty Waitress, or Ditzy Cheerleader, or, well, you get the point. Except for a sitcom that got cancelled after one season. Right, well, shockingly, that's not what I dreamed of doing. I love dramatic roles. I write. I think I might be pretty good, too. And I was just starting to break in as something other than slutty set dressing, *just* starting to get taken seriously as a writer."

She was looking down at the ground now, digging her feet into the grass, her voice sad. He wished he could fix it for her.

"I was just starting to believe I could really do it, you know?" she said, looking up at him so he could see her eyes were wet. "And now I'm a fucking punch line."

Chance was starting to put together what was happening, and knew he had only a few minutes to make a decision. If she really needed his help, he wouldn't be able to turn her away.

"Look," she went on, "I'm aware of how crazy this is. We just met yesterday, technically. And part of what's messing me up is how I was so dumb to trust someone like Richie."

Chance shrugged. "Be fair to yourself. We

had a hell of a day yesterday."

"You going to let me finish?" she said, throwing a clump of grass at him.

"Might as well." He grinned back. "But I'm warning you, you keep talking to me like that, and you're going to earn yourself a paddling."

"A paddling?"

"Or similar."

She looked at him, wide-eyed, like she couldn't tell if he was serious. Let her figure out that he was. She must know he was a Dom—the only reason he hadn't taken her over his knee already was that he wasn't sure if she knew what it meant.

"I hate that you've seen the pictures," she said suddenly. "That you've seen me like that. Because that's not—"

"I haven't," Chance said, forcefully. "No. I told you I wouldn't, and I didn't."

"Then how did you know?"

"Someone suggested to me what they contained, and who the man was. That's all."

An eyebrow went up. "Suggested what they contained?"

No way in hell he was telling her that a thirteen year old had found them on the internet. It's not like she didn't know that was happening, but she didn't need it thrown in her face, either.

"Lena, I don't care what's in the photos. I care that they hurt you. You don't have to tell me about them."

"Yes, I do," she said, standing up a little straighter. "He had me tied up in chains. He had a whip. Or a flogger? There are some photos where I'm flogging him. I didn't really like that. There are…toys. And honestly, after that, I'm not really sure. I couldn't go through all of them. I doubt I ever will."

She was looking him dead in the eye, like she needed to prove something. He had no idea what. She had to know that none of that shocked him. The only thing he cared about was that she'd been hurt—and *that* made him crazy.

"Lena, what are you getting at?"

"I'm telling you all of this because I don't want you to think I'm stupid. I mean, I can understand, right? Like, how could I not be at least a little bit stupid if I was with Richie? If I let Richie do things like that to me. What I'm trying to say…"

She took one more deep breath, and what Chance would remember is that he could see her shoulders shaking. That she was really that nervous. Her little golden shoulders were shaking while she clasped her hands together, looked right at him, and told him what she needed.

"I was never hesitant about the kinky stuff. I was hesitant about Richie. Because I've always been into the kinky stuff. I've always…I've always been curious. And I've always wanted to learn, but there's never been anyone to teach me. Richie's bullshit has taken so much from me, Chance, it's taken my career, it's taken what little ability I still had to believe that most people aren't complete assholes. I won't let him take this from me, too. I need to keep this. I need to own it. And you're the only man I trust, Chance, because you turned me away, even when you wanted me. Because you did what you thought was best for me. I don't care what terrible thing you think you did in the past, or if you've broken other girls' hearts. I'm not looking for your heart. Trust me, mine is messed up, too. I need you to help me own this, Chance. That's why I came here tonight. I need you to help me become a submissive. Please…help me."

chapter 7

Oh God, I can't believe I said it.

Lena was suspended in this horrible moment in time, right after those words left her mouth, when she didn't know what he would do or what he would say. She could understand why he rejected her before. She was a woman in a rough spot, he was a (mostly) good guy, and that's kind of a weird don't-go-there situation.

But now she'd just poured her heart out. She'd just said things she'd never even said to herself. And then she'd begged him.

She'd *begged*.

"Oh my God, Chance. Please say something."

He stood there, only steps in front of her, but so far away. He had an unreadable expression, like he was having trouble processing what she'd said. Or like he was weighing the pros and cons. She couldn't bear it if he said no. It would just be the final straw.

Had she been wrong? Every time she got near him there was this crackling fire, this unheard of static in the air that made her feel...she didn't have words for it. She'd been *sure* he'd felt it, too.

And then she saw him. The jaw, pulsing. The shoulders squared. Those *eyes*, flashing. Staring straight at her.

His voice was low and rough. "I'll help you," he said.

Lena might have been embarrassed by how relieved she was to hear that if she hadn't been overwhelmed by the immediate thought of what came next.

With the sight of Chance, a solid column of sculpted muscle, advancing toward her.

"Ok," she said, feeling nervous again, so nervous, light and skittish and fluttery. Now it was happening. Really, really happening. She wasn't some inexperienced virgin, and she would never have described herself as shy — ever — so what the hell was this? Her eyes strayed downward, unable to meet that blue stare, and she was captivated by a light dusting of fine hair running down his chest, his abs, all the way to his belt...

She licked her lips. "Ok, so, how do we, you

know…I mean, I'm on birth control, and I have test results, and I've heard that you guys are super strict about that, which, obviously, is awesome. And I mean, I don't, like…have equipment…"

Stop babbling, dummy!

Her voice faded as his much larger body crowded hers and she gave in to the sheer physical presence of the man. It was beyond words. Her ability to articulate evaporated before the expansion and contraction of his chest, his ribcage, his abs, with every breath, with the male scent of him, now so close, overwhelming her senses. Some part of her that clung to a sense of control flailed and panicked. Would she know what to do? Can you fail at being a submissive?

"I don't know what to do. I mean, do I call you 'sir?' Do you tie me up? Do—"

"Later," he said, his voice curt and strong.

He didn't want to talk anymore.

The muscles in his neck twisted and turned as he looked her over. She could feel the heat of his eyes on her, like he was devouring her with that gaze, inch by slow inch. She swore she could actually, for real, *feel* it, her skin sparking alive in the wake of that, whatever it was he was doing to her without even touching her. She was aching and swollen, already, beginning to burn hot.

Suddenly his hand was in her hair, her head

pulled back, his eyes on hers. She couldn't move if she wanted to, held in place by his grip, and as he touched his rough fingers to her cheek she actually felt her eyelids flutter. He ran his hand down her neck, her breasts, around her waist, never taking his eyes off of her, and by the time he'd stopped she was breathing hard, panting, fucking *panting*, and her panties were soaked.

Chance kissed her. No, he claimed her. Rough, hungry, hard. She melted. Her arms around his neck, desperate already to have him on her, in her, whatever he was going to do to her. He moved down, nipping at her neck, and, with a satisfied growl, reached his long arms down to grab the hem of her dress.

And removed it.

Pulled it up, over. For a moment she clung to his neck instinctively, but he unwrapped her arms, held them high above her head, and the dress was gone. *Gone.*

This was insane. She felt safe with a man she barely knew, safe enough to do this? And yet she wanted it. She *needed* it.

Her chest shuddered with ragged, uneven breaths as he bent down again, his eyes on her still, the look of raw, determined need on his face bringing her even higher. His hands roamed everywhere. Like he was mapping out his territory. He fell to his knees, his hands moving faster and faster, his mouth on her breasts, her belly, and then he bit her hip. A low sound tore from his throat and he thrust his hand between her legs and pulled her thong down to her ankles. Lena felt her legs buckle and somehow he caught her, folded her in his arms, and spread her on the grass.

He stood up only long enough to take his clothes off.

Oh God. Every inch of him, hard, chiseled. Muscles sliding under his skin as he moved, the telltale ripple of abs leading her eye down to the most unbelievably perfect cock she'd ever seen, standing hard and erect.

A beat. A moment when their eyes locked. And Lena knew, as if she didn't already, that this time wasn't about abstract power games or rules or scenes. Just dominance, in the most primal, feral way. The two of them wanting each other beyond all thought or reason. This was just…animal.

He was an animal.

He fell on her like a hunter, his mouth searching out her nipples, her neck, her lips, but he held back what she wanted most; hovered over her, just out of reach, as she wrapped her legs around him. She mewled, pulled at him, scrabbled at his back and shoulders, working herself into a frenzy of driving, primitive need, her hips rising off the soft grass, feeling nothing but the dull ache that was the absence of where he should be.

Chance reared back and slipped his hands under her ass, picking her up off the ground. She arched at just the anticipation, clawing at the grass under her fingers while he pinned her with those eyes.

He never looked away.

His fingers dug into the soft flesh of her hips as he pulled her onto him while he pushed forward, impaling her slowly on his full length, eyes boring into her while he filled her completely. He was big. Big enough that it hurt a little, even with how slick, how wet, how *ready* she was, and holy shit, she liked that, too.

"Look at me," he demanded. As if she could do anything else. She felt herself clench around him, her core bearing down on him as what promised to be a massively strong orgasm built inside her, and the ripples flowed up through her abs, her chest, down her arms and legs, into her fingers and toes.

"Oh God," she heard herself moan. "Please..."

He slid in and out of her with deliberate slowness, prolonging the delicious feeling of tension growing inside of her. Torture. Pure torture. She reached forward for him again, just wanting *more*, not even thinking coherently, but he caught her hands.

Chance leaned forward, pushing farther inside her, and pinning her hands to the ground.

"I am in control of this," he said. "Always. That is how this works. You are mine. Your body," he said, pulling out and then pounding into her, "is *mine*."

His eyes seemed to glow, staring into hers, and his words filled her with satisfaction as he drove into her again and again. Her whole body seemed to sing.

"Yes," she said, wide-eyed and frankly amazed. She'd agreed to this, she'd *asked* for this, but still she couldn't help but think, *What the hell is happening?*

"Mine to fuck," he said, thrusting into her again, "mine to punish, mine to make come. Fucking say it."

"Yours," she panted, almost delirious now, "*Yours.*"

She meant it. Whatever the hell this was, Chance holding her down and fucking her mercilessly, owning her, wanting her to know he had total dominion over her — *yes to all of it*. This was what she wanted, what she hadn't had with anyone else. Nobody else made her feel safe enough to let go. She was helpless to resist.

"Mine," he rasped.

He dragged the head of his cock over her g-spot and picked up the tempo, driving her higher and higher, every thrust punctuating his point, his *ownership*. Just thinking the word sent a shot of pleasure through her and it put her over the top. She clenched around him so hard she heard him grunt, her back arching so high off the ground that she felt possessed, her legs pumping, every fiber of her being gathering together for one moment before she evaporated into a million points of light.

She let out a wild, ongoing scream, and he never, never stopped. One hand holding her hands above her head now, the other free to fondle, tease, torment.

"Look at me," he said, and she could hear it in his voice, strained, tight. He was close. That thought sent her spinning upwards again, and the look on his face while he watched her made her feel like nothing else. Beautiful. Wanted. Safe. Helpless. His. This man who she'd just met, who seemed to know her body better than she did, who she'd begged to submit to. The man was an artist with his hips, his strokes hitting her most sensitive nerves, his thumb teasing a nipple, his eyes, his *eyes*, seeing right through her, all the time.

"Come," he said, driving into her hard, and she did, *again*, her muscles finding some way to flood her with pleasure, with *him*. Like her body already knew obedience, like she was meant for this, with him.

He came with her, watching her, his thick, heavy cock twitching inside her, his huge body shuddering, his thick fingers digging deep into the turf. The feeling of his orgasm on her, in her, shattered her. When she came up for air she felt warm and languid, relaxed and full.

Chance.

He lay on top of her, muscles uncoiling, coming back down. The scent of him was overwhelmingly sexy, and it was all over her. His weight on her—in her, still—felt just as right while he breathed hard into her neck. She could feel him relax, muscle by muscle, and she ran her hands over every part of him she could reach, just checking, over and over again: *mine*. Whatever conversations they would have, whatever rules there were, however this actually worked, right now, in a rooftop garden surrounded by countless tiny lights, she was certain she had made the right decision. His body was hers, too, for however long this lasted.

She wanted him again. She wanted as much as she could get. She couldn't imagine being sated.

How? How was that possible?

"Chance," she said.

He didn't speak, but pushed himself up on strong arms, impossibly thick in the dull light, leaning back on his knees to look at her. She actually mourned a little as he pulled out, but man, she loved watching him. The muscular planes of his torso were slick with sweat, shining in the light of the garden. And she loved the way he was looking at her, like he couldn't believe what he had in front of him, like he was thinking already of all the things he was going to do to her.

"Beautiful," he said.

He slipped an arm under her and scooped her up just as easily as if she were weightless. A new amazing sensation hit her: she was being carried by Chance. She buried her face in his neck, drunk on his scent, and ran her hands over his buzzed head.

"Where are we going?" she asked. Her voice was almost starting to sound normal again.

"More," he said.

She felt a smile spread across her face and nuzzled deeper into his neck as he carried her to...wherever, she didn't even care. Knowing he wanted her as much as she'd wanted him, as she still wanted him, was intoxicating.

Feeling his erection press into her again, already, was something else.

He kicked open a door and carried her into a dark room. It took a moment for eyes to begin to adjust, and she realized she was thrilled at the idea of not being able to see, not panicked. That was new.

That, apparently, was Chance.

He navigated the room in the dark, from memory—his suite? He'd mentioned a suite. Her suspicions were confirmed when he lowered her onto cool, soft sheets, and then dragged her back towards him, so that her bottom was balanced just on the edge of the bed.

"Lie back," he said. "Hands at your sides. Grab hold of the sheets."

She did as he told her, surprised at how free she felt while following orders. It shouldn't make sense, but somehow...

She felt his hands around her ankles, and then he was lifting and spreading her legs again, positioning himself between them. She smiled and gave a satisfied little murmur. She was going to get expertly fucked again.

"Stay still, Lena," he said, now a huge shadow that loomed over her. She was enjoying this element of the unknown so much that she almost didn't want her eyes to adjust—except that she was missing out on seeing that beautiful man. "Whatever I do, you keep your hands where they are, you understand?"

A small shiver raced down her spine. His voice was different. Fuller. Deeper. It didn't even occur to her to argue or disagree.

"Yes," she said. "Sir."

She was rewarded for that with a little growl, and a hand on her breast, fondling her nipple. "I've wanted you since the moment I saw you, Lena. I'm gonna be at this for a while."

"I have no problem with that," she breathed.

"You might, later," he said, leaning over

her. God, she loved the feel of him on top of her. "I have an appetite for you like you wouldn't believe."

Oh, she would. She could see herself becoming a Chance addict. Just one time, and…

Her thoughts were interrupted by his finger sliding inside her, curling around to coax a moan from her.

"That's better," he said, much closer to her now, hovering right over her. His finger kept dipping in and out, lightly caressing her inside and out. Teasing her.

"Please," she said, and her hips said the rest.

She heard him laugh. "You think that's begging?" he said.

She might have come back with some smart ass remark—and part of her lingered on what he might have done about *that*, his words "mine to punish" still fresh in her mind—but he covered her lips with his. The kiss started gently, though his finger never let up, keeping the pressure inside her building steadily. He parted her lips with his tongue and, good God, was there anything the man couldn't do well? His tongue was just the right amount of pressure, just the right amount of moisture. And when he bit her bottom lip, she found herself clenching.

"Interesting," he murmured.

And then his mouth was gone. He moved to

her neck, her earlobe, her collarbone, her shoulder. Her nipples ached for his attention, hard, fierce little points, but he took his time with that tongue.

God, that tongue.

What else could he do with it?

"Chance," she said.

He answered by taking one nipple in his mouth, and pushing another finger inside her. His hot, wet tongue toyed with her nipple while his fingers pressed upwards, inside her, right on her g-spot. Her body wound tighter, coiling in a knot around that very spot, and her desire to have his cock inside her again turned into a very pressing need.

"Chance," she said again, and his teeth closed around her peaked nipple. It *hurt*.

And she liked it.

"Oh God," she said again, this time to no one in particular. The universe, maybe? Her hands twisted the sheets around her as she stared up into the dark and his tongue trailed down her stomach.

Three fingers inside her now. Getting fucked by Chance's hand was better than anyone else she'd had.

"So wet," he said. "So beautiful."

"Chance, *please...*"

"You should see what you look like when you come," he said, ignoring her. She could feel his breath on her thighs. "Fucking amazing."

"*Chance…*"

"Don't move those hands," he warned her.

A fourth finger. Oh God, now she felt stretched so wide, and the pressure was too much…

She felt his lips close around her clit and groaned. His tongue started slow, laving wet circles around her clit while his fingers—his *hand*—started to fuck her in earnest, curling up to her g-spot with every stroke. She was certain she was going to lose her mind. Another cry tore from her throat, and it didn't sound human, even to her, and then he put his lips around her clit and sucked.

She didn't know what tore through her. Crashed into her. For one horrible moment she thought she was going to pee, out of nowhere, and then she came with such violence that it actually hurt. It swept over her like a giant, overwhelming wave, drowning her in nothing but that white, incandescent sensation, obliterating everything in its path. The contractions whipped her about the bed, sheets tangled, legs cramping around his shoulders.

She was flooded with it, and it took a while—she had no idea how long—for it to recede. She felt Chance lick her thigh and kiss her stomach, murmuring something. He sounded fevered, urgent. She lifted her head, barely, still somehow weak, and shifted her bottom.

It was wet.

Oh God. She hadn't imagined that. She had really…

She met his eyes, humiliated and embarrassed, not quite sure what she had done, expecting to find him — what, grossed out? Or worse, pretending to be fine with it?

"You are fucking amazing," he said.

"I'm *so* sorry —"

He rose to cup her face with his hands, forcing her to look directly at him. He didn't look disgusted, or annoyed. He looked hungry. Ravenous. Like he'd only just started.

"Don't ever apologize for an orgasm like that," he said. He was actually breathing hard. She could feel his dick pressed against her, and he was rock hard.

"I'm so embarrassed. It felt like I had to pee, but I don't…"

He smiled, laughed, kissed her. "No, you didn't pee. That was female ejaculation. That was the most beautiful fucking thing I've ever seen."

He really…he was really smiling. Like she'd given him a gift. Softly, she said, "I've never done that before."

His grin now was wolfish. "How'd it feel?"

Her turn to smile.

"Are you sore?"

"No, I'm ok."

"Good," he said, lifting her leg. "I'm not done."

By the time he was, she was too tired to get up. Too tired to talk. Too tired to do anything but sink into sleep, lying peacefully on Chance's chest, feeling like she'd been thoroughly, irrevocably marked.

chapter 8

Chance woke up in the exact same position in which he'd fallen asleep: with a peaceful Lena sleeping on his chest, like a kitten.

Good God, *Lena*.

His brain, his body, on fire with Lena.

Better than he'd imagined. Than any man alive had a right to hope.

He tried to rein himself in and think about the fact that he'd made a promise, meaning he had an actual obligation. This wasn't just empty fucking. She trusted him to help her. In the back of his mind, as he was advancing on her, scouting her body, taking in everything he could, he'd wondered if he'd feel the same way the next day, that this was his only choice, given what she'd said. Or if he'd wake up knowing he'd made a promise he couldn't keep to someone who needed help.

So far, so good.

He'd walked up those stairs convinced that he would explain some things, that would be that, and she'd be on her way.

And then she'd said the one thing that could have compelled him to change his mind. He did not see that one coming, that was for sure. Once she'd said she needed his help as a Dom to get over what that idiot did to her, he was just a goner, no hope for him at all. As a Dom, first of all, he couldn't turn away a sub that needed his help. But it was like she knew he'd spent the last few years reliving the times he'd failed a woman who needed his help, and knew he'd make up for it in any way he could.

Except she didn't know any of that. She couldn't. And thinking about Jennie or the Asala family again should set him on edge, like it always did. Only now he had a naked Lena draped over him, and he felt...

In control. Normally he only felt like that in the topspace of dominating a sub, usually in a scene. It was that same feeling he'd had earlier, like just her presence calmed him, took off that edge in him that was always looking for a bad guy to fight.

He frowned. That was dangerous freaking thinking, right there. Chance knew enough to know that no one else was going to fix him but him. That wasn't how people worked, and looking for that in someone else was as bad as a woman who thought she could fix a broken man and got herself into a bad situation as a result.

Focus on the present. Focus on what you promised her you'd do.

Well, at the present moment, he was very much enjoying the prospect of Lena in his bed for the foreseeable future. And the prospect of keeping her naked for as long as he wanted.

He smiled. Good thing it was his prerogative to set the rules. It was good to be a Dom.

But first things first. He needed confirmation that this was the right thing for her. He needed to hear it in the light of day, and he needed her to hear his own reservations—informed consent wasn't just some byword. He'd need it before he broke out the toys or set any rules.

Slowly and carefully, so he wouldn't wake her, he shifted Lena onto her side, next to him. She only sighed, and settled down on to her back, giving him an unbelievable view.

Damn, she had to be cute when she was sleeping, too.

Chance pulled on an old pair of sweats, then padded to the bathroom and got a warm, wet washcloth, which he then wrung out and brought back to the bed. They had made a considerable mess. Normally he wouldn't just pass out without cleaning up, but that night had been anything but normal. Still, it was his job to take care of her, no matter what the outcome of their coming conversation. No woman went neglected in his bed.

So he'd take care of her.

He climbed back onto the bed and gently began to wipe her down with the washcloth. Didn't take long for *that* to wake her up.

But she woke up smiling.

"That feels good," she murmured.

He bent her leg at the knee so he could get to her inner thigh, and she opened her eyes with alarm. Then she tried to hide it.

Interesting.

"What are you doing?" she asked, leaning up on her elbows.

He grinned. "Cleaning you off so I can mess you up again," he said. "If I decide that's the way to go."

Her cheeks darkened. God, she was beautiful.

"I like you on me," she said quietly.

Chance paused. She hadn't said that seductively, or teasingly, or…anything but quietly and earnestly. He was instantly hard. He looked up to see if she was retreating from that little unplanned moment of vulnerability, and yup, sure enough, she wouldn't meet his eyes now.

"Are you sore?" he asked.

She shook her head, mute.

He said, "Last night was something."

"Amazing," she murmured.

"Yeah, it was. It was also what we might call off the books," he said, running the washcloth up her leg. He heard her breathing quicken. "Not part of our official arrangement. That will begin today, conditional upon a few things."

Her eyes went wary. Chance gently stroked her with the washcloth while he met her eyes, wanting her to get the message: he'd take care of her, no matter what.

"What do you mean?"

"Easy, sweetheart," he said. "Don't get spooked. This is a big thing you want to do, and I need to make sure you know what you're getting into, and that you're doing it for the right reasons. I'm cautious because I don't want you to get hurt. Ok?"

She visibly relaxed, but not all the way. What had she expected the conditions to be — something he wanted from her? Like she expected him to take his pound of flesh?

Yeah, she had some issues to work out.

"Ok," she said, eyes still a bit narrowed. She pulled herself up so that she was leaning against the headboard, and pulled her legs up to her chest. Covering herself in a protective stance, defensive as hell, however unconscious. That wouldn't fly when — if — they got started, but now wasn't the time to go at her defenses head on.

She said, "So what conditions?"

"Well, first things first: before we get into what it would mean for me to train you as your Dom, you need to know what I was going to tell you last night," he said, feeling…strange. He should have the tightness in his gut, the feeling running up and down his spine, just thinking about this.

He didn't. He was just focused on her. The Zen of Lena.

Chance trapped her with his stare, wanting her to know that this was important.

"I don't know what image you have of Doms. If it's from books and movies or even the internet, it's probably wrong. Or at least not one hundred percent right."

"Strangely, as an actress and a writer, I am familiar with the concept of fiction," she said, smiling slightly. She seemed relieved, her shoulders dropping another fraction of an inch. On familiar ground. Good.

Give her a preview.

Chance grabbed hold of her foot and rubbed it in his hands, chuckling. "Just you wait 'til you find out what I'd do to my sub for that kind of smartass remark."

Her sudden intake of breath was definitely noticeable, her skin flushed, her pupils dilated. Chance smiled at her, not gently, but hungrily, and kept going.

"Look, Doms aren't cartoon-perfect, though some of them like to think they are. I'm a man who's sexually dominant, and damn good at it, but I have flaws, like any other man. Big flaws. And I have a past full of fuck ups, though *not* involving BDSM," he added. "It's important that you know that. I have my own demons, Lena, and that's why I was reluctant to get involved with you. The only way I normally get involved with women, and with submissive women, is no strings attached, and you…"

He sighed. He had her full attention.

"You've got some strings on you."

"I do, do I?"

"You know you do."

She tried to stare him down. Chance might have laughed, but he didn't want to hurt her. He waited until she looked down, her long black eyelashes fluttering prettily on those smooth cheeks—just like a good sub.

"Listen," he said, rubbing her foot with tender care. She was starting to relax under his touch, which was a good sign. "This—what you've asked me for? This is different. I take my duty as a Dom very, very seriously. I take that responsibility seriously. I take it so seriously that I take my ego out of it. It's the most important thing in my world, and while I train you—*if* I train you, Lena—you become the most important thing in my world. It won't be about me until I think you're ready for it, though, trust me, I'll look forward to that day," he said, letting his mind drift briefly over all the ways he would take Lena for his pleasure. "But until then, it'll be about you. Do you know what you're getting into?"

"I think so," she said, braving a look up. When she saw his face, she smiled, brightening up the room. "You sound like me—you come with a warning label. I think I might have been weirded out if you *didn't* warn me about something. Those guys who think they're perfect are usually the ones you have to worry about."

Would wonders never cease? His crazy, beautiful, untrained sub was *smart*, too.

"What's your warning label?" he asked, stretching her leg out toward him. She was opening up, slowly.

She laughed, and it was shiny, glittering sound. "Irrevocably skittish? Oh, and prone to trusting the wrong people. So that's a good sign, right, Mr. Guy I Inexplicably Trust?"

Lena was laughing at herself as she sat before him, naked, and let him massage her leg, working his way up, but that didn't mean she wasn't still scared. Chance could feel it, an undercurrent working between them, some part of her silently asking him for reassurance.

He was used to reading subs. He wasn't used to feeling this...connected. Not right away.

"Yeah, you do trust me," he said. "Why?"

"I told you last night."

"Not good enough. This is serious stuff. Answer me."

He had stopped toying with her now, needing to get to the heart of this, and he could see her struggle. Good. She was putting effort into it, treating it seriously. If she hadn't, he would have reconsidered everything.

"I can't give you a solid answer," she said finally, meeting his eyes. "And that bothers me at least as much as it bothers you. In the end, I just...do. Part of it is the way you looked out for me yesterday. Part of it is how Adra spoke about you, about your reputation. Part of it is Volare's reputation. Part of it is what I felt last night. What I feel right now," she said, taking a deep breath that seemed to reverberate throughout her whole body.

Chance was sure he felt it, too.

"But I'm not dumb," she went on. "I know none of those things should be enough. It just feels right. And," she said, "before you say anything, believe me: I think that's crazier than you do, given what I've just been through. But I'm tired of missing out on things in life because I can't trust that they'll turn out perfectly. For some reason I trust you for this, and I am reveling in the novelty of that feeling. Besides, if you turn out to be an axe murderer,

I..."

He raised an eyebrow.

She stopped, cocked her head, laughed. "I was about to say I don't have anything else to lose, but an axe murderer would be going after heads, right? That...that would count as a loss. I retract the axe murderer comparison."

"Formally?" he asked. This woman was just *fun*.

"Formally. Provided you're as sane as everyone thinks you are, I don't have anything else to lose."

Well, he'd been there. To him it didn't signify weakness or even desperation— sometimes rock bottom was where you found yourself.

In fact, Chance was beyond pleased. He hadn't expected that. Not at all. Not with the whirlwind nature of this whole thing. But that had been an intelligent, thought out, considered answer, honest and realistic, and even a little insightful. It had been everything he might hope for in a potential sub.

"I'm glad you said that," he said. "I can train you, as nuts as this has been."

"I didn't know I was being interviewed!"

She tried to kick him and he caught her easily, dragging her body down to his and spreading her legs just enough.

He saw her breath hitch and her lips part.

"I told you, I'm going to be assessing your

needs," he said, holding off just a little longer. "But more importantly, Lena, this stuff is serious. I need you to be honest with me like that all the time."

"Well, that should be easy with all this insane trust."

For a moment Chance was just lost, staring at her. She had relaxed into her new position, her breasts just perfect and beautiful and wanting to be kissed, her legs long and lean, her eyes shining, her smile easy.

This whole thing was just so...easy.

And she was looking at him in just the same way.

"You know I was worried I would wake up this morning and think this was a huge mistake," she said.

Chance feigned surprise, as though he hadn't had that exact same thought, then gave her that wicked grin again. "Do you?" he asked.

"No. For some...again, inexplicable reason." Lena pushed her foot into his lap, a little playfully, a lot provocatively. He was hard all over again. "This stuff gets explained eventually, right? Or is it just going to be one long mystery?"

"Oh, you're going to be explaining things to me," he said, running his hand up her thigh. "Whatever I want. You'll answer my questions. You'll obey my orders. Fundamentally, you are giving up control. Do you understand that?"

He stopped with his hand just over her sex, just resting on top of it, not moving, studying her face, her body, her eyes for any sign of reluctance. None. Just a slight fear, the kind that heightened her excitement, and…gratitude.

"Yes," she whispered.

"Good. Now we talk about the terms of our arrangement," he said.

And he slipped a finger inside her.

She let out a small sound of surprise and blinked, her wetness flowing over his hand.

"We need terms?" she asked. She was playing it cool, but her nipples were starting to tighten into pretty little buds, and he could see her start to swell.

"Hell yeah, we do," he said, moving in slow circles inside her. "We're gonna be doing some kinky stuff. You've gotta be clear on the rules going in. Safety is paramount, Lena."

"That's good to hear," she said.

Her head was back on the pillow now, and her eyes were closed. She was sinking into the pleasure away from him. That wouldn't fly. He leaned forward and slipped another finger into her.

"Oh!" She arched into his hand.

"Look at me, Lena," he ordered. "You don't come without me unless I tell you to, you get me? You don't go off into your own private headspace unless that's part of the scene. So you look at me. And right now? You aren't coming until I tell you to."

"But—"

"No. I want your full, undivided attention," he said, moving ever so slowly, just enough to torment her. "Consider it an incentive."

She glared at him. He was enjoying this too damn much.

"Ok," she breathed. "What…what are the rules?"

"I'm gonna give you a checklist later to look over, but right now, can you think of any redlines you have? Stuff you just can't do?"

"I don't know."

"You know what a safeword is?"

"Yes."

"Ok, well, think of it like a stoplight. Green, yellow, red. It's my job to read you, but I'm not telepathic, so when I check in, you answer me. If you can't answer me because you're deep in subspace and have just spaced the eff out, I'm stopping. You're not sure, need to take it slow, need to check in? Yellow. Red—"

"Means stop."

He stopped his fingers. She frowned a little.

"And we're gonna have to work on your manners, Lena," he said. "Don't try to talk over a Dom, sweetheart. Not this Dom. Not in this arrangement."

"Ok," she said. "What happens if I do?"

Just the suggestion of a glint in her eye. This one had a spark, but he knew that already, didn't he?

"Discipline. Punishment."

Her breath quickened again and she tightened around him. "What does that mean?"

"What I decide it means."

She was squirming under him a bit, and he doubted she even knew it. So that was interesting.

"I'll be figuring out what you need, what you respond to, what you avoid. We're gonna find out what kind of sub you are, and what you want. But that means we have to explore. That part isn't always fun."

"Good thing I trust you for this."

Lena locked eyes with him again, bracing herself while she moved her hips ever so slightly, her hands twisted up in his sheets.

"Uh huh, because while it might not be practical to make you go naked *all* of the time," he said, smiling as her eyes widened, "or keep you tied to my bed at all times, we'll compromise."

Oh man, he felt her get even wetter. His erection was starting to get painful.

"Compromise?" she said. Her voice had gotten breathy and her hips had started to move.

He decided to see how far she'd go. Push

that button.

"Lena," he said sharply. "Look at me. You will always be sexually available to me. All times, all places. At any moment, I might give you the order."

Everything stopped — except her, clenching around his fingers.

"The order?"

"If I tell you to take off your panties and bend over, you'd better do it."

She laughed, he guessed from embarrassment at how much that turned her on. She was as easy to read as a book, especially with his finger inside her. It was tough to keep his face stern. Even tougher not to just take her again right then.

"Ok," she said, biting her lip.

Ok. He was glad to see that his instincts about her were still dead on. That was kind of a big play right out the gate, and she was still playing along with him.

"Most things I'm gonna be doing for your benefit, Lena," he said, moving his finger a bit faster. "But some stuff I'm gonna do just because I want to."

"Yes," she said, panting. "I am totally in favor of that."

"Hey, what'd I say? Don't you close your eyes," he said. "I didn't say you could —"

"But I'm so close, Chance," she said, looking him dead in the eye.

He immediately ceased fucking her with his fingers.

Well. He wasn't wrong about that, either. She was already testing one of his rules, closing her eyes and talking over him to see what discipline meant. This one might be into provoking funishment without even knowing the word. Some Doms hated that sort of game, but Chance had always been a playful guy, just as long as it was on the up and up. And just his amazing luck to get a precocious, beautiful, responsive sub. Too bad she was being manipulative.

Well, time for her to learn.

"Now, I'm only telling you this because you're new," he said, keeping his voice easy. She'd learn hard in a minute. "But I suspect that you just broke a rule intentionally."

"Yeah?" She was grinning now. The minx. He made a mental note.

"Yup. Lotsa Doms hate that, you know. Can be considered very manipulative. Topping from the bottom. And in this case I suspect it was. I'm open to most things, so long as we all know where we stand. But what happens next kinda depends on whether you're honest about it."

"What depends?"

"Whether you get funishment, or punishment."

Now her eyes widened even more, her

pupils dilated, and he heard her gasp — and she didn't exhale. Scared and aroused. Good combination for personal discovery. He got up off the bed and looked down at her. Time for the voice.

"Get up," he ordered.

She sat up so fast she seemed to almost forget that she was naked. But she obeyed instinctively, responding to his tone. Another good sign.

"Don't cover yourself around me."

She dropped her hands to her sides. Her breasts trembled as the rest of her body just barely shook.

"Get up and walk over to the bench." He pointed at it. He could tell she hadn't made sense of anything in his bedroom the previous night, which was to be expected. Now he could see her take in the sight of a spanking bench in real time. "It's exactly what you think it is, Lena. Don't make me tell you again."

She hesitated a little, her uncertainty coming through her gait as she walked to the bench. She reached out and touched it briefly before looking back at him.

"Put your knees in the stirrups and bend over the bench."

He saw her throat move as she swallowed, and he bet that if he put a finger to her neck her pulse would be racing. So far, so good. No safewords. True submissive.

"*Now*, Lena."

She snapped into motion, getting her knees into the stirrups with more dignity than most. She only hesitated again when it came time to bend over. He'd seen that expression before — disbelief, like she was expecting something else to happen. If she had serious misgivings about submission, now was when it would come out. But he didn't think she did. Chance was sure she was about to discover something amazing about herself.

"Lena," he said severely, "When I give you an order, I expect to be obeyed. We just went over this."

He put one hand on the back of her neck and pushed her down onto the bench. He heard a small sound escape her lips, but she only put up token resistance.

"Grab the handles you see in front of you."

She did.

Now he took a moment to enjoy the view. Every inch of Lena's body was beautiful, as far as he was concerned, fit and soft and not too thin, but her ass was, frankly, a work of art. He ran his hand from the back of her knee up the back of her thigh and watched her shiver, then let his fingers dance around her pink folds peeking through. She was so wet it was like she was glazed, the morning light reflecting off of her damp thighs like an invitation. He turned the crank that adjusted the position of the stirrups and spread her legs a little bit.

But first things first.

He kept a firm grip on the back of her neck, knowing it sent a primal message of control.

"Lena, did you break my rules on purpose?"

A small sound. A chirp? He laughed.

"I can't hear you, Lena."

"Yes, I broke your rules on purpose. Sir."

His cock jumped at that. *Sir*. He liked the way she said it.

"Why?" he demanded.

"I wanted to see what would happen."

Thwack. He spanked her across the meatiest part of her ass and watched her jump in surprise. He kept his hand securely on the back of her neck and held her down through that first instinct to struggle. And that made her flush even more.

She liked force. He'd get to ravish her eventually.

He looked forward to it.

"That was a mild blow for punishment, for your reference. They get harder. You could have asked for more details. Why did you provoke me?"

When she spoke this time, the breathiness was back in her voice.

"I thought it would be fun."

Chance smiled. A girl after his own heart, for sure. And if he were not mistaken—and he wasn't—that spanking itself had turned her on.

He ran his hand over the globes of her ass and down to her very wet, very slick folds.

Way the hell turned on.

"That's honest," he said. "Good girl. Five blows for the original infraction—you're getting off light, you hear me? Next time it's gonna really hurt."

"Yes, sir."

Thwack. Thwack. Thwack. He varied up the rhythm and the intensity, watching Lena closely to see how she'd respond. Her physical response was undeniable, but he'd only be certain about her psychological response after she talked to him.

Thwack.

She moaned and writhed at the same time, as much as she could. He'd seen this combination before—arousal, slight pain, humiliation, all of it drawing out the endorphins that led to release—but never in quite so lovely a presentation.

He let his hand rest gently on her bottom, and caressed the skin. She wouldn't have a mark on her.

She was panting, though.

"Lena," he said. "You may get up."

He'd removed his hand. Lena didn't move.

"Lena," he said, not bothering to hide his amusement, "Do you want to get up?"

"…No."

"Why not?"

"I don't know."

He put his hand on her back and stroked her. He could see her begin to relax.

"Confused?"

"Yes. I'm sorry."

She truly did want to please.

"Tell me what you're feeling, sweetheart. That's a rule, too."

"It was...a rush. But now...I don't..." She turned her head to look at him, her eyes heavy, her lips swollen. God. So it wasn't shame, then. "I don't have words for it yet."

Chance stroked her, feeling the heat underneath his palm grow. He swept his hand down her back, over the perfect curve and between her legs. He palmed her and asked, "Do you want this?"

Her breathing was ragged and she looked up at him, almost begging.

Almost.

"Yes," she said.

"And this?" he said, pushing his middle finger deep inside her. She gasped—bent over like this, she was wide open.

"Yes," she whimpered. "Chance, please."

"Please what?" he said, his tone hard.

Lena swallowed.

"Please fuck me."

chapter 9

Chance's dick was throbbing, but he had total self-control in this kind of situation. He wouldn't do anything to endanger a sub who maybe didn't know her own limits, especially not this one. He needed to be sure. Nothing about this situation conformed to the usual training dynamic. But he was the only one she felt she could trust. He felt like he had to reinvent the wheel.

"You have to find the words, Lena," he said.

"You want me to beg?"

"Convince me you know what you're asking for, and why."

Goddamn, this would be easier on him if he hadn't looked. Dark red, swollen, wet.

"Shit!" she said. He laughed. Good to know they were both frustrated. "I've always fantasized about this, but this was…I don't know. It was like breaking through something, going higher," she said. "Better than high. I need it. I need to know."

"You hoped I'd spank you when you acted out."

"Yes!"

"Then it's not a punishment. I could leave you like this. Engorged, aching. Leave you like this with no relief."

"Oh, please, Chance," she said.

"Convince me!" he barked.

She was silent a moment. Perhaps really giving it some thought. Her thighs were quivering and he stroked her there, calming her while she did her best. He could see she was trying. He would support her.

"I'm sorry," she said finally. "You said it could be manipulative. I was…that was manipulative. Disrespectful. A terrible thing to do."

She turned her head, looked over her shoulder at him.

"I really am sorry," she said, and the look of sadness on her face tugged at him. "I should have just asked you, I just didn't…I guess it's not easy for me to do that yet. I won't do this again, I promise."

Chance brushed her cheek with the back of his hand. He felt immense pride in her. Hell, he'd been proud of her just for having the guts to come ask him to train her, but somehow it hadn't clicked until now what an essentially brave person she was. She had the courage that was a prerequisite of integrity—you needed courage to look at your own actions and be honest with yourself about them. Not one in ten people had it.

"Apology accepted. Next time, you really will be punished. This time, I want to reinforce how important it is to be honest and aware. You get that?"

He walked around behind her and cranked the stirrups a bit wider.

"Oh my God," she breathed. "Yes."

She actually lifted her ass toward him. He smiled, and shook his head at the sight in front of him. Perfect. He wanted to reward her for her honesty, for the effort that went into it, for making progress.

But first…

"*Now* I want you to beg," he said.

He saw her head drop down in anguish, and her body strained for him. He gripped her hips to let her know where he was, and pushed the head of his painfully swollen cock just inside her.

"Oh God," she said. "Chance, *please*."

"Not good enough."

Thank God she couldn't see his face. Every primitive urge in his male body was telling him to plunge into the unbelievably ready

119

female in front of him. He had perfect control of himself when it came to women, but damn, his face would be intense right about now. He could feel a vein in his forehead throbbing.

"Chance, please fuck me. *Please.* I need you—"

He surged forward and buried himself to the base in Lena. He felt the wet warmth of her wash over him, and felt her muscles contract around him immediately, and everything was *right.*

"Oh *God,*" she cried, and she angled up to him, moving back and forth on her knees while he held her hips and pounded into her. She was so hot, so wet, so soft—and already so close to coming.

Something about taking a woman from behind always brought out the wildman in him, and he leaned forward to grab the back of her neck, driving his cock into her with enough force to make her cry out with each thrust.

"Oh God," she screamed. "Fuck, *yes…*"

And that was the last word he heard. She screamed as she came around him hard, so hard he yelled into her back, held her down, and thrust until the tension rushed to his center, squeezing his balls like a vise, and exploded out in dizzying currents of pleasure.

He collapsed onto her back, both of them too spent to move, stuck together with sweat. Chance could feel his pulse throughout his entire body, throbbing away like a dull echo of that orgasm.

Jesus.

This woman…there was nothing like this woman.

Chance forced himself up even though he felt somewhat drained, which was also a novel experience for him, at least on this scale. But he needed to take care of Lena, so up he went.

She whined as he carefully pulled out of her, giving him another reason to smile.

"Stay right where you are, and I'll be right back," he said, placing a quick kiss on the back of her neck. She murmured something, her body draped over the bench like she was ready to take a quick nap. He wished he could let her do exactly that, but there were some unresolved issues. First and foremost, Paul Cigna.

Chance already knew what his call would be. That guy set off a number of alarm bells and he was not going to stop. But Lena needed to come to that realization, too.

Still, it was a lot to put on her on day one. Then again, nothing about this had been typical so far. They just had to roll with it.

First he got another warm cloth and cleaned the both of them up, taking great care with Lena's tender flesh.

"You sore?" he asked her.

"Dunno."

He grinned. Still in outer space.

After he'd gently rubbed some oil into her thighs and buttocks, he slipped one arm under her torso and lifted her, slowly, from the bench, catching her as she rose up and scooping her into his arms.

"I can walk, Chance," she said. "I was just being lazy."

"Nope," he said. "I'm gonna hold on to you 'til I'm sure you're recovered. And because after I fuck you, I like to hold you."

She didn't say anything to that, but he felt her eyes on him. After a moment, she leaned her head into his chest, and he felt her body relax into it.

"I'm ok with that," she said.

He carried her to his favorite chair, a beat-up, giant green velvet-covered monstrosity that was the most comfortable place in the world, and very carefully situated her on his lap. She was a natural snuggler.

Chance slid his hand to her chest to feel her heartbeat. It was slowing down, and her breathing only jumped when he touched her. Good.

"Your brain working properly yet, sweetheart?" he asked, enjoying the scent of her hair.

"I think so."

"Good. There are a few things we should

talk about."

She groaned, and he couldn't hide his laughter with her head right on his chest.

"Like, a...*talk*, talk?" she said. She tried to sound casual, but she wasn't. That, too, was interesting. She was able to compartmentalize her ability to trust, and to become vulnerable: she was good with him for BDSM activities, but not so good with the idea of emotional commitments.

More than that, though, she was just so damn sensitive. He could feel the anxiety start to build within her just from not knowing what was coming. He hated to see that happen under any circumstances.

"No," he said, "though freaking out about that means we'll be coming back to it. We have to talk about the Paul Cigna situation."

"Who's Paul Cigna?"

"You remember the jerkwad in the blue fedora?"

She stiffened. "How could I forget? What a dumb signature piece. It's the only way I'll ever think of him."

"He came by my gym yesterday with some questions about you," he said, keeping his voice calm and casual. "About us, in fact."

Lena pushed herself off his chest and looked at him with some awful combination of fear and anger and general freaked-outedness.

"Are you serious?" she said.

"Whoa, Lena," he said, and pulled her back against him. "Yeah, I'm serious, but try not to get too stressed. Do me a favor and trust me on this. Just let me do my thing."

She had become a big ball of tension in just a few seconds. She'd have to constantly feel under assault to have that kind of reaction. Chance was going to apply physical comfort before he discussed the issue with her, but now he realized she probably wouldn't begin to unwind until she felt in control of the situation. Or at least until it was under someone's control.

"Ok, Lena," he said softly. He was stroking her arm and her back, slowly and rhythmically, the kind of thing she couldn't help but respond to. "We'll deal with it. He didn't get anything, and he's not going to. I won't allow it. But while he's still looking, I'd like you to stay here."

There was a silence. Finally, she said, "With you?"

Chance frowned. He heard that note of wariness in her voice, like maybe he was turning this into something that didn't feel quite as safe to her. Lena expected things to turn on her at any given moment. She wasn't kidding when she had said this whole pictures thing had messed with her head, but he was starting to think it might run a little deeper.

"You'd have your own room, with a lock.

And with a writing desk. You can have your pick of any of the ones that are still free, just until you feel like you can go back to your place without worrying about that idiot jumping out of the bushes."

Those assurances seemed to work. He could feel the tension ebb out of her body, and she pulled her head off his chest long enough to give him a naughty smile.

"But not *too* far from your bed, right?"

"The entire world is my bed as far as you're concerned, remember?"

She bit her lip, color rushing into her cheeks. "I do."

chapter 10

Lena let the cold water rush over her, hoping it might clear her mind. She wasn't having much luck with it so far.

It wasn't even afternoon yet, but she was feeling...she didn't know the word for it. Not exhausted — though, man, that would be an issue soon; was the man an Olympic athlete? — but perhaps emotionally strained. She had been in emotional lockdown mode since the pictures broke, and, if she were being honest, since well before that. She'd picked a career that was full of rejection, and her personal life hadn't been much easier, even as a kid. Learning how to ignore certain feelings had been a necessary survival mechanism for her.

Now she had to not only feel everything all the time, she had to be aware of them and of what they meant. And she had to tell Chance all about it.

She understood the reasons for it, intellectually. But emotionally she was feeling like she'd gone from being a couch potato to running a marathon.

She was going to be a bit sore.

And that's what she tried to tell herself this was, as she stood in Chance's oversized shower, trying to wash away her worries. Just overtraining for someone with out-of-shape emotional muscles. And for someone who'd had sex more times in the past twenty-four hours than she'd thought possible. Something about their physical connection made it seem...normal. Inevitable. Irresistible. And it wasn't just the physical connection, either—the fact that they got along so well, that seemed to have similar sense of humor, that they just *got* each other, it was all having an effect on her judgment.

And the result was that somehow when he'd held her in his arms, stroking her back like she was a frightened stray—which, ok, actually really did help—the suggestion to stay at Volare until this whole thing blew over had made sense. It had even started to seem fun. Desirable. Relaxing.

Now? She was stressing out like nobody's business. Chance had left her in his suite while he went and got some of her stuff from her apartment. She hadn't wanted to face the possibility of dealing with Paul Cigna or any of his stalkerazzi buddies, so Chance had offered.

And she'd *agreed*. Sure, man-I-just-started-sleeping-with in a bizarre arrangement, go to my apartment and get my things.

So why was she flipping out about staying at Volare now?

It felt so…intimate. But really, it was just a room. Maybe it was because it was Chance who felt so close to her, already, and she had good reasons to be worried about that. She knew the guy wasn't available for a real relationship. That was part of what had made this arrangement seem like such a good idea in the first place. She didn't have to worry about getting involved only to find out that he was secretly a terrible person, or using her for something, or any of the other ways she'd had relationships end. But that was before they'd had sex. That was before she'd felt…

Whatever this was. That connection, maybe. A physical connection like nothing else she'd ever experienced.

Which, when she put it like that, seemed like a good thing for what she wanted out of this: someone she could trust who could help her learn about her kinks. But it carried with it the risk of falling for the man. And not only would that obviously not work for Chance, but it wasn't like Lena had the best track record in that department, either.

The idea of being vulnerable to him—to anyone—in that way had sent her right into a panic attack. Hence the cold water.

Was she supposed to be honest with him about this, too? That just was not going to happen. Some boundaries needed to be kept, for both their sakes. She wasn't going to mess this opportunity up because she asked too much of him.

Like going to get her stuff by himself?

Damn.

She hadn't even called Thea to warn her that he was coming!

"Oh, what is wrong with you," she muttered to herself while she hastily toweled off. She managed to find her phone in only a few minutes, which, considering the previous night's activities, was something of a miracle.

"C'mon, Thea," she said. It had rung altogether too many times.

"I was wondering when you were going to call me," Thea's voice squawked from the speaker. No greeting for her. Right to the point, as always. Lena smiled.

"Sorry," she said. "I was a little distracted."

"Yeah, I would be, too, in your shoes. Speaking of which, you know that man is actually packing up your shoes as we speak?"

He was packing her shoes? Shoes, plural?

"Yeah, I'm sorry. I should have called you to

tell you he was coming, I just...I've had a lot on my mind."

"Your *mind*? Then you don't know what to do with that boy. Besides, he called me first. Good manners on that one."

"Trust me, I don't need to hear any more about his wonderful qualities," Lena said. She was still in a towel, and realized she wouldn't have any other clothes until Chance came back. Still, she wanted to be useful. She could at least strip the bed.

"Lena, honey, gossip and bragging aside, please do tell me something about what's going on. I worry in my dotage."

What had she *ever* done without Thea?

"Um, so. God, I don't know why this is so awkward, but...he's helping me with something."

"Is he your Master?"

Lena stood bolt upright, letting her towel fall around her ankles, the sheets only half stripped. "My *what*?" she said as she struggled to recover any towel-based dignity she had left.

"Yeah, I'm not dumb, honey, and I've been sexually adventurous for more years than you've been alive. Plus, we have the internet now. Makes it very easy to check up on people."

"Jesus, Thea."

"I'm not judging. I don't know if it would be

my cup of tea, mind you, but you never know until you try."

"No, he's not my…master. Well, I don't think so. But he is, um, teaching me, I guess. I just didn't want to let Richie take that from me, too, and Chance is…Chance has been amazing."

"I bet." There was a pause, very uncharacteristic of Thea. When she spoke again, her voice was softer. "I'm proud of you, honey, for doing this despite that bastard Richie. You get yours, you hear me? I want to see you happy."

Lena felt tears gather in her eyes. Why should she cry? It was a *good* thing to be loved by your family, even if you'd had to move halfway across the country and get kicked out of your last apartment to find them. Thea was the one person in her life who had never let her down. Sometimes Lena didn't quite believe she was real.

"Chance thinks I should stay here for a little while, at least until that photographer bozo gives up and leaves me alone," Lena said. "But I won't if you don't want me to. It's not really a big deal."

"Oh, he told me. And don't be silly. It's only temporary, and I like living on my own. I did it for years before I met you, remember? You're the exception, my dear, and I will be glad to have you back, but in the meantime I'm gonna cook naked as much as I want."

"That doesn't sound remotely safe."

"I like to live on the edge."

"See, this is why I worry about you alone," Lena laughed.

"Well, I won't be alone as long as this 'photographer bozo' is here to keep me company."

A chill passed through her, taking any levity out of the moment. She had thought about Paul Cigna as an abstract threat, but the way Thea talked about him made him seem very real.

"Thea," she said carefully, "do you mean that he's there *now*? The guy who was wearing that goofy hat? The skinny, rat-faced one?"

"Distinctive, isn't he? I'm afraid so. I've seen him every time I've been out. It's just him, though, none of those others have been back."

Which was actually much worse, in a way. It meant that Lena had been right in her initial assessment—she just wasn't that interesting to most tabloids. The kink, Richie's status as a former child star, and her looks had been the selling points, but L.A. had no shortage of good-looking people doing stupid things on camera, and most of them were actually famous. Photos of her would probably only bring in decent cash in the day or two after the original photos leaked, and that's if they brought something *more* to the story—like the insinuation that she was dating Chance.

It meant that Paul Cigna was out on his own without much hope of taking a lucrative photo. It meant that Paul Cigna had reasons of his own for stalking her.

For making her feel afraid.

What an asshole.

"Lena, honey? You still there?" Thea sounded worried.

"Yes. I'm just pissed off," she said.

Which was so much better than being anxious or afraid.

Hadn't Chance already taught her that? That the best way to stop feeling like a victim was to fight back? She had knots in her stomach at the thought of Paul Cigna still staking out her house. Forcing her into hiding. Bothering Thea, no matter how much Thea pretended it didn't matter. No matter what Chance did to help her feel better, in the end, this tiny, terrible little man called Paul Cigna would always be able to make her feel hunted and powerless, just by showing up.

If he wasn't just doing it for the money, he might be dangerous. But what if he was? What if there was some angle she didn't know about?

Couldn't she just end it now? And know, once and for all, what Cigna was really after. Just the idea of *knowing* calmed her down. At least then she could plan. It would simplify her life—and it might simplify things with Chance. He wouldn't feel obligated to do all this above and beyond stuff for her sake, and she wouldn't be afraid of becoming dependent upon him. And Chance would definitely appreciate her wanting to take back control of her life. Maybe learning how to submit and give up control in very controlled situations was just the other side of this same coin.

Lena had seen how pleased he'd been when she'd braved through difficult questions. And something about pleasing him felt right—as right as fighting back.

"Thea, can you see the weasel out there?"

"Yup. He's in his car, an old, beat-up brown Volvo, just down the block. Watching."

"Ok. I'm going to deal with this right now."

"Lena? What are you doing?"

"Give me two minutes."

It took her at least that long to find her clothes from the night before, clothes that had apparently been favored with the same miracle that had blessed her phone: barely wrinkled, no grass stains. She toweled off her hair, pulled on her tight white dress, which, in full daylight was maybe a little hooker-y, and slipped into her heels.

It felt like battle armor.

chapter 11

Thea had hovered for a while as Chance packed Lena's stuff into his old Army duffle, even remarking on how most women wouldn't let a man they'd only just started sleeping with anywhere near their private things, but eventually she'd seemed satisfied with his conduct. He was being careful, after all. And he wouldn't know about most women — it occurred to him that he'd never done anything as ordinarily intimate as pack a woman's clothing for her before. It just hadn't come up.

Huh.

Even so, Thea had eventually wandered off to take a phone call, and Chance had been left in Lena's apartment. The clothing had been easy; she had a nice closet, easily organized. He'd gotten that out of the way in about two minutes, even though he was sure to have screwed something up, but he figured he could take her shopping.

Damn, this was moving fast. From zero to sub in one day.

Anyway it was the other essentials he was having trouble with, reminding him how much he didn't know about this woman he inexplicably — to use her word — felt close to.

Her apartment was full of books. Just everywhere they could be stashed, books. Well-loved books.

And not just books. There were legal pads with dense handwriting all over the place, bulletin boards with index cards on them with little headings like, "Inciting Incident: car wreck" or "Plot Point 1: gets the package." He had no idea what they meant, but apparently Lena did, and this was obviously all important to her. She wasn't kidding: she wrote like it was her job.

He couldn't take *all* of it, not yet. But he obviously had to bring some of it. A woman who lived and breathed books and writing like this obviously needed them. He could just check out these binders to find out which one was the script she was working on now, and bring that over with her laptop.

He hadn't meant to start reading. But he had to at least skim to figure out what was current.

Then he'd gotten sucked in.

Somehow she'd made the story of two lovers on opposite sides of a war funny and breathtaking and heart wrenching. And *suspenseful*. He wasn't a guy who read romances or love stories or whatever, but this was crazy. No wonder no one knew what to make of her stuff. It was unlike anything else, and it was just too good.

The thing that got him, though, was her grasp of people. He'd only ever felt like this when reading *Anna Karenina* back in high school. That was the only book in that long, torturous year of Ms. Grisham's English class that had blown his mind. Maybe it was the burgeoning Dom in him, but he'd been fascinated by how Tolstoy had so much empathy and compassion for people he didn't even like that he was able to get inside their heads completely. Tolstoy *knew* his countrymen, better than they knew themselves.

This was like that.

He laughed—he'd just compared Lena to Tolstoy. That…that was insane, right? Chance was no literary critic, but he knew what he liked. Screw it. Tolstoy it was.

That was when Thea had shouted for him.

He shoved a few of the binders and her laptop case in the duffel, slung it over his shoulder, and headed toward the commotion.

"Thea, what's up?" he called down the

stairs.

"I think our girl might be doing something a little crazy," she said. "I only tell you this because I don't know if that photographer is the violent type, and because you run faster than I do."

Chance had seen Paul Cigna sitting in his car down the block. Apparently, so had Lena.

He broke into a run, tearing out the front door.

Lena was definitely doing something...maybe not completely crazy. But not obviously sane, either.

She was standing at Cigna's window, blocking the photographer's view of Chance's approach, dressed in her outfit from last night and yelling something.

Shit.

Something in Chance redlined. That man was intent on hurting Lena, either psychologically, with his fucking camera, or physically, because he was a creep. Chance welcomed the feeling he'd learned to hate—that lurch in his gut, the fire coursing up his spine—because it was what was going to stand between Lena and Paul Cigna. He broke into a run.

"Let's just get this over with so I can get on with my life," Lena was saying. "I'm not interesting, I'm not famous, nobody cares who

I'm dating or what I'm doing, so why don't you take whatever creepy ass picture you want right now and then leave me alone?"

Chance was close enough now to hear Cigna's creepy, calm response.

"But that's not the shot I want, sweet thing."

The beast in Chance roared.

Keep a handle on it.

Chance put a gentle hand on Lena's elbow and firmly pulled her out of Paul Cigna's line of sight. He'd be damned if he let that asshole enjoy the view of Lena in that dress for one more second. When she saw it was him, she unconsciously stepped into the protection of his arm, and in the back of his mind he was pleased.

But first things first.

"Hey, asshole," Chance said, leaning down to the window, feeling like he could get his fingers to leave dents in the metal if he wanted. "What did I tell you last time?"

Cigna's expression turned on a dime. The fear on the man's face as he put his car in gear was satisfying, though not as satisfying as it would have been if he'd begged Lena for forgiveness and promised to leave her alone—on his knees. Instead, the coward peeled out without a word, turning recklessly onto Abbot Kinney.

Chance held Lena close to his body and took deep breaths while he waited for the pressure inside to dissipate and be replaced by normal thoughts. He was still on high alert.

He was still pissed about the leer he'd seen on Paul Cigna's face, and not just because the man himself sickened him—he had been leering at a woman who was his. His responsibility.

"You ok?" he asked Lena, looking down. She was still pissed, but ~~she~~ there was something more—she looked puzzled.

"I'm frustrated," she said. "And confused."

Frustrated? Confused?

Did she have any idea what kind of danger she'd just put herself in?

"Lena," Chance said, keeping his voice controlled. "That could have been dangerous. I get why you'd want to confront him, but don't do that again. I'm not kidding."

She raised a mischievous eyebrow. "You're not the boss of—"

His look stopped her. She said, "Oh."

"Yes," he said. "I am."

"Yeah, but not literally."

Jesus, this woman. Chance stopped her, put the duffel down, and turned her to face him. They were in the middle of the street, and he did not give a damn.

"Yes. Literally, figuratively, however you want to put it. Your safety is my responsibility—physically, psychologically, whatever. All of it. I am not going to let anyone hurt you, not Paul Cigna, not you. That clear?"

Lena's head had been back at the confrontation with Cigna, but now she was most definitely in the moment. She looked up at Chance with some weird mixture of nervousness, happiness, and that anxious tension he'd seen in her before.

"Yes, that's clear," she said. "I didn't…I didn't think of it like that, though. I just wanted to take control of it. I thought you'd be pleased. And I *was* pleased—it felt good. Until he got, you know, all creepy."

Were her eyes actually brimming with tears? Sensitive, brave, wild submissive. It was every flavor he loved, and now she was crying because she'd disappointed him, or because she thought he was being unfair, or both, when she was already in the middle of an emotional time.

But she needed to understand this. He sighed.

"You notice things, don't you?" he said. "You noticed I was proud of you when you pushed yourself. And I encouraged you to take control of that situation yesterday. And it felt good when you did."

Lena nodded, clearly embarrassed that she was nearly crying. He tilted her chin up so she couldn't avoid his gaze.

"Look at me," he said. "I am proud of you for wanting to fight, and don't beat yourself up for crying—you've got a lot on your plate. But your safety is always going to come first. You put yourself in danger on my watch again, and I'll have you over my knee in the damn street, you understand?"

The shock of his promise hit her physically. He watched her closely. First a look of gratitude, so much gratitude just because he cared even a little bit—again, she expected so little of him, maybe of everyone. Then outrage.

And then it all gave way to arousal. Arousal crowded only by the lingering expression of shame.

If he didn't think it would be too much for her at this particular moment, he would have pulled up that dress and spanked her in the street. The thought drove him crazy.

As it stood, he didn't want her to feel insecure about their arrangement, he just wanted her to think before she did things, but he wasn't good with words the way she was. He did better with actions.

He grabbed her by the waist and took her mouth in his, the first touch of her tongue reigniting his hunger for her all over again. It never really went away, but just touching her was enough to make him burn for her, brighter each time. She tasted so sweet, and yielded to him so well, giving back with just the right touch of pressure, just the right sensation on her lips…

It was just supposed to be a little possessive kiss, something reassuring, but it needed more. He pressed her to him so he could feel her breasts on his chest, fisted his hand in her hair, and took his fill. When he felt her skin go hot he pulled away, licked her bottom lip, and let her go.

"Ok?" he asked.

Lena smiled faintly, her fingers going to her swollen lips. She seemed a little dazed. "Um, yes. Ok. Definitely ok."

"Ok. Now that's settled, tell me why you were confused back there, before I get distracted by that body in that dress. At least until we get in the door."

"What?" she said.

Chance smiled to himself. Yeah, she had that effect on him, too. Good to see her get a taste of her own medicine.

"You said Cigna confused you, sweetheart."

"Oh, right. Well, I just wanted to get it over with, you know? So I was like, 'Just take the freaking picture, get it done, I'm standing right here.' But he didn't want a close up or whatever picture I offered him. He was taking photos as I walked up to him, but it was like he was taking B roll."

"What's B roll?" he asked as he walked her back to Volare.

That got a smile. Hell, if it got a smile like that every time, he'd sign up for a full education in Lena's school of L.A. knowhow.

"It's like in documentaries. When some expert's talking about an artist, for example, they show B roll of the artist at work, because five minutes of watching *anyone* talk is insanely boring. So they shoot the guy mixing paint, or preparing his canvas, or literally anything related that's more interesting than a talking head—all of that is B roll. And for still photography, sometimes they'll do candids. Like, everyday life."

Chance looked down, his mind turning her explanation over, trying to figure out why that worried her.

"So what's his A roll?" he asked, holding the gate open for her.

"Exactly," she said. He thought he saw her shiver.

chapter 12

Lena glared at the blinking cursor on her laptop and tried very hard to ignore her phone. It was, she was sure, mocking her. Her laptop was full of good things: her work, her progress. Her phone…

That was something else. Her phone had become the enemy.

For lack of a better word, she'd been inspired since coming to stay at Volare. Something about the energy of the place, and the energy of Chance—and the energy that Chance put into her, on an impressively frequent basis—made her feel completely uninhibited. Or as uninhibited as she was ever likely to feel, anyway. The result had been a burst of creative brilliance where she'd figured out the major problems in her latest screenplay and had set out to rewrite the entire thing, top to bottom. In only a few weeks. And now she only had one key scene left.

So why couldn't she write it?

It wasn't because she was worried about any of the usual things. This had been like a dream vacation. She wasn't worried about her career; she hadn't been online in forever and she wasn't even thinking about money, though she knew she probably needed to kind of soon. But when she was with Chance, when she was hanging out with Adra, playing pool with Ford, the club's blond-haired, gorgeous lawyer, or meeting any of the other people in this incredible place, she felt accepted, at home, relaxed. Small miracle, really. She would actually let down her guard.

Until she'd get another text.

There had only been a few of them, and she didn't want to make a big deal out of it, not only because she was still mindful of the boundaries of her arrangement with Chance, but because, frankly, she didn't *want* them to be a big deal.

But she did wonder how Paul Cigna had gotten her phone number. She assumed it was Paul, anyway. She didn't want to think about whether there could be anyone else in the mix.

He would run out of steam soon. She was sure of it.

And in the meantime, he wasn't going to

ruin what she had going here. Because for all the rancid, foul speculation about her personal life outside the Volare compound walls, this whole venture had changed her. Was changing her.

Chance was changing her, in all the ways she'd hoped he would.

She'd never been more sexually fulfilled. There hadn't been as much of the whips and chains as she'd thought there'd be, at least not yet—it felt like he was getting her used to being controlled. And she wasn't just getting used to it, she was getting to love it. She felt like she was more of herself now that he'd allowed her to become fully her.

He'd made every effort to get to know her. Lena was very conscious of constantly being under his surveillance, even while trying to respect her privacy, of how he looked for clues to her hang-ups and desires in every thing they did together—watching her favorite movies (he'd sat through *Thelma and Louise* and he'd laughed all the way through *The Producers*), playing scrabble, going to a batting cage, whatever. Whenever she caught him looking at her like that, it felt like foreplay. And it felt more and more like she was right to feel like she could trust him.

In fact, at this point, just the thought of the man got her wet. And the fact that he'd *told* her that would happen? That he'd get a freaking

Pavlovian response out of her? That he could eventually get her to come on command?

She squirmed in her seat and tried not to smile. No way she was getting a dramatic scene done now.

"Almost done?"

It was Chance. He stood leaning against the open door of her little writing room, his plain white shirt stretched tight over his shoulders, his arms crossed and his eyes smiling. God, even his muscles had muscles. Lena kind of spaced out at the sight of him for a moment before she remembered all the notes she had all over the office he had given her.

Yeah. He'd given her an office.

Which she was actually insanely protective of.

"Oh man, please don't ask," she said, unaccountably embarrassed. She scrambled to flip over note cards and close her laptop, stowing it at her feet as though people might telepathically read her work if they could see it. She knew it was nuts. It was even more nuts because it was Chance who'd had the foresight to bring some of her writing stuff over, sparing her another encounter with Paul Cigna, which was achingly sweet. "It makes me crazy to talk about stuff I'm working on while I'm working on it. I know it doesn't make any sense, but it just *is*."

"That's pretty cute, you know that?"

She scowled at him.

"Was that a look?" he asked, eyes bright.

Uh oh. Honesty, or…?

"Maybe," she said.

Chance pushed himself off the doorframe with no apparent effort and walked towards her. He pulled her chair aside and crowded her until her butt bumped against the desk behind her.

He had that look again. That hungry, dominant look.

Her body betrayed her entirely. Her nipples hardened into little peaks, visible even through her bra, and if she thought she was wet *before*…

Chance bent his head with a quick, athletic grace, and she heard him inhale.

He was smelling her.

"You are sweet," he said lazily, his head coming back up. "Take off your shirt."

Lena's blood rushed south, but her eyes immediately went to the open door behind him. It was really, really open. She could see the hallway circling around the open space looking down on the first floor below, the floating staircase on the opposite side, even into another room on the other side of the building. And if she could see out, anybody could see in.

Chance had told her this was a possibility, but they hadn't done anything in public yet. Not even in public places in Volare.

She smiled, uncertain. "Don't you want to have dinner first? Aren't you hungry?"

"Ate already. Want to play with you. Take it off."

Play with her. Just the way he said it, like she was his to toy with, whenever he wanted, wherever he wanted—her clit throbbed ever so slightly.

Well, she was, wasn't she? She had agreed to that.

A small rumble in his chest got her attention. She quickly pulled her comfy old Led Zeppelin shirt over her head, looked up at Chance wearing only her black bra and a pencil skirt, and rode the sensation of adrenaline flooding her system.

Then she held her breath.

"All of it," he said, frowning slightly, and with one quick twist undid her bra clasp. Her breasts bounced free while he pulled the straps over her shoulders, and just the movement, and the look in his eyes as he watched them move, made her clench.

"Do you know how hot these are?" he said. "How insanely fuckable you are?"

Chance played with both breasts, rolling her nipples in his fingers, kneading the soft mounds in his hands. He knew how sensitive she was there and knew just what to do with that information. She gasped, licked her lips, and tried to keep her head.

"Chance, you know the door is open."

His eyes flicked up to her face, blazing with lust. "Of course I know," he said.

Deep. Full. Dom.

"But—"

"Strip," he said, taking a step back.

She got little chills from that voice. She only hesitated a little bit, but in that moment she took her eyes off him for an instant, looking at the direct line of sight between her and just…so many places in Volare, with that freaking door open…

"Lena," he said. "I'm giving you the order. *Now*."

Oh my God, oh my God, oh my God.

She'd fantasized about this. She hadn't tried to get him to do it, not only since that would take all the fun out of it, but also because of what he'd taught her about manipulating Doms. But fantasy was so, so different from reality. From knowing she was in plain sight.

Then why were panties already soaked?

She closed her eyes. "Yes, sir."

And stripped off her skirt and underwear in one movement, like ripping off a bandaid.

"Eyes open."

She obeyed. His eyes killed her every time. Like there was absolutely no point in hiding anything from him. She was already feeling lightheaded, a sign that she was about to start floating off into what he'd called "subspace," and he'd barely even touched her.

"Sit on the edge of the desk."

She pushed some papers out of the way, thinking how silly it had been to be embarrassed about them compared to what was happening now, and perched on the edge of the antique sanded wooden desk. She jumped when the lip of the desktop pressed into her bottom, putting sharp pressure on her already swollen sex. Her skin started to heat up, and she knew she was blushing, or as close to it as she could get.

Chance fondled a breast while he smiled at her. "Spread your legs for me. Keep 'em that way."

Lena knew better than to check the door again, but she couldn't help it. Chance pinched her nipple, hard.

"Sorry," she said hurriedly, and spread her legs as wide as they would go, hooking one leg over the corner of the desk.

Chance whistled low.

The air was cool on her exposed, wet folds, and her nipples had started to ache from want. She was breathing so fast she really was lightheaded now. She didn't dare look at the door again, but it was there, in her peripheral vision. Open.

And then someone walked by. Someone tall. Male. She couldn't tell from the corner of her eye if they'd looked or who they were...

"Oh God, Chance, they can *see*," she said.

"Yup. But I don't think you get how you feel about that yet," he said, and dipped one finger inside her, quick in and out, the sudden invasion forcing a moan from her. He held the finger up in front of her, where she could see that it was shiny and slick with *her*.

"You see what I mean?" he said, grinning at her.

Bad man. Bad, sexy, impossible man.

"Touch yourself," he ordered. "Make yourself come for me."

Her mouth fell open a little. This was new. She couldn't remember the last time she'd felt ok doing that in front of someone. If ever.

Lena's throat felt dry, but she swallowed her fear and locked eyes with Chance. That right there sent little tendrils of pleasure curling through her core, and she licked her lips. Nobody made her feel like this. Nobody made it this easy.

Slowly, she trailed her fingers down her abdomen, the muscles fluttering under her own touch just because it was Chance who demanded it, until she found her center. Oh God, was she ready for him. She reached her middle finger inside herself to wet it, and when she saw Chance's reaction, her own muscles tightened.

"Do it," he said, his voice husky.

His eyes fell to her exposed sex, and the

muscles in his neck corded while he flexed his jaw. She knew that if she looked down she'd see he was hard. Bulging through his jeans. The thought of his large cock, hard and ready for her, drove her fingers to her clit. That first touch, with Chance's eyes on her, sent a tremor through her.

She moaned.

"Faster," he demanded.

Lena obeyed, rubbing her clitoral hood over the highly sensitive bundle of nerves, each stroke pushing her higher. With her eyes half closed she took a deep breath, the spread of oxygen igniting pleasure in every nerve, and moaned.

"Yes," Chance said. "Come for me. Now."

And he reached up and pinched both her nipples, hard, pushing her over the edge into an entirely different kind of orgasm. Her scream strangled in her throat, her mouth hung open in a kind of shock, her eyes half rolled back in her head, and her abs jerked her forward, into his arms.

chapter 13

Holy mother of God, would you look at that.

Chance wasn't easily shocked anymore, hadn't been in a long time. But watching Lena pleasure herself had left him awed. To see her unfold before him like that, each layer more beautiful than the last, and to know she did it for him? It set his body on fire.

He'd been feeling her out for the past few weeks, gently prodding and pushing, assessing her needs, conditioning her to his control. She didn't need much conditioning—she responded beautifully—but Chance wanted to make sure he had the right approach for her. So he'd been figuring out where her emotional land mines lay and how best to confront them before they delved into more intense scenes. He could sense already that her reticence and difficulty with certain things went beyond what Richie Kerns and Paul Cigna had done to her, even though the damage from that seemed to be somehow ongoing. He'd had a hunch about the vulnerability of public display, or even the hint of it, and it had paid off.

There was something deeper at play. He'd get to it.

But right now he was overwhelmed with the sight below him. With the smell of her.

Lena's beautiful honey skin was darkened with pleasure, her chest rising and falling with big, air-sucking breaths, her heart beating fast under his hand. She'd fallen forward into his arms and he'd gently lowered her onto the desk, keeping his palm on her chest to calm her and keep the connection between them.

Her nipples were wine dark red where he'd pinched them.

She was fundamentally gorgeous, splayed out there for him like that. Hell, all the time. And it was only about to get better.

"Lena," he said, putting his free hand between her legs. She'd instinctively draped one leg over the corner of the desk and the other over his shoulder, giving him full access.

Good girl.

When he rubbed the pad of his thumb gently over her clit, she moaned — in pleasure, not pain. She was no longer oversensitive in the aftermath.

Good.

"Look at me," he said, unbuttoning his jeans.

She propped herself up on one elbow, still a little shaky, and opened her eyes. Immediately she looked at his heavy cock, thick and hard after what he'd just seen, and throbbing in his hand. The greedy look on her face made him twitch. He stroked himself once and then positioned the head right at her entrance, nestled in her inner lips.

Jesus, still so wet.

Lena's chest heaved, with those beautiful breasts bouncing slightly, beckoning him.

"Oh God, yes," she said, looking up at him with eager eyes.

He pushed her back down until she was flat on the desk and moved the head of his cock in slow, excruciating circles around her entrance.

"Stay down, Lena," he said. He wouldn't tease her for long. Just long enough to get the point across.

"Yes, sir," she said, just a hint of a smile on her lips. He grinned. Just the kind of sub he liked.

"I know what you need now, Lena," he said, sinking into her, watching her chest rise as her back arched in slow, slow time with him. Her breasts were trembling by the time he was fully seated inside her. What a sight.

"Yes, *sir*," she breathed.

Her hips rolled rhythmically, begging him to move. He grabbed hold of them with his big hands instead, his thumbs angled up toward her waist and his fingers wrapping around to her ass. He had a solid hold on her. She wasn't moving without his say-so.

Lena knew it, too. She groaned.

"Look at me," he ordered.

Those hazel eyes always held him. Always.

He pulled out slowly, saying, "Introduction is over. After this, we're gonna get started." He watched her eyes widen, wondering what he meant, and then he slammed into her.

She yelped, fingers clawing at the papers on the desk while she squeezed around him like a warm, velvet fist. He watched her face while he fucked her with hard, deep strokes, slowly at first, picking up the tempo as her face twisted in that rictus of painful pleasure that he loved to see. There was nothing like fucking Lena.

He lifted her bottom off the desk and angled into her as deep as she would let him go and watched her cry out, her breasts bouncing with every thrust, her ass quivering in his hands. Her legs kicked out, finding no purchase or leverage, reminding her how helpless she was in his hands, and he swore he could *see* that take her to the next level. It spurred him on to fuck her mercilessly, reveling in the fact that she could always take it as hard as he could give it, and when her orgasm started to take her, kicking and writhing and running from and to the sensation at the same time; it was so strong that he felt like he was being sucked inside her whole. She shuddered as she contracted around his dick, and the look on her face sent him into orbit, emptying all of himself into her in one last, powerful thrust.

He leaned on her in the aftermath, his own knees going weak for a second there. When he finally had the strength to push off and clean them up as best he could, he just stared at her for a second, lying there in the late afternoon sun, still a little sweaty, her hair mussed around her face. His shining girl.

"You ok?" he asked, running his hands down her body, wanting her to know he was still close.

"Mmmm."

He smiled. Damn, she looked good like that. Deliciously ravished.

"What do you say?" he asked.

She opened her eyes and sighed contentedly. "Thank you, sir."

Chance was finding it hard to look away, but he knew if he kept looking at her like she was, knowing he'd done that, knowing he could do it again, well...he would. If Lena wanted to, she could make him hard until it hurt and he begged for her to stop.

"C'mere," he said, pulling her up off of the

desk so he could hold her. She complained briefly, but then relaxed into his arms.

"You feel good," she said.

He smoothed her hair down and kissed the top of her head. "You wouldn't believe how you feel," he said. "You are so damn beautiful, it hurts, I swear."

She put her arms around him and squeezed. "Keep talking."

"I see you're not so focused on that open door anymore, are you?" he laughed.

She didn't say anything, only nuzzled his chest.

Chance always took good care of his subs afterward, like any decent Dom would, but with Lena it was just as good, in its way, as sex. He'd come to look forward to it.

"Hey, weren't you supposed to be somewhere?" she asked.

He had told her he'd be gone for part of the afternoon—he was still training Michael, though he wasn't sure Billy knew about Volare, and he'd planned to talk to the man about it. But his time with Lena had gone on a little longer than he'd expected. He'd be later than usual for Mike, but it wasn't like the kid was going anywhere. He'd just do his summer school homework until Chance got there.

"Yeah, I'll go when we're done," he said.

"Don't do that," she said, pushing off of his chest. It took her a moment to find all of her clothes, but she dressed quickly. "You had plans."

He frowned. This was setting off his Dom sense.

"Taking care of you afterwards is more important," he said, pulling her to face him. "You're important. And using the imperative with me is not so wise, sweetheart."

She gave him an uneven smile, not that bright, blinding thing he always looked for, and put a delicate hand on his chest.

"I'm fine," she said. "You should do the things you want to do. Where are you going?"

Chance put a hand on her cheek and saw that something about the idea of him changing his plans to suit her really bothered her. Which meant he'd have to revisit it later and find out why. But not now, when her defenses were up—again.

"I'm going to the gym," he said, and slapped her hip. "Be ready for me when I come back."

The look she gave him as he left was priceless.

~ * ~ * ~

Lena couldn't believe Chance was going to go work out. The man was some sort of genetic freak with endurance like that.

Not that she minded.

She did get a little nervous when he seemed intent on staying, but it passed. It was the same panic she'd felt in the shower when she'd agreed to stay at Volare, the same thing she always felt whenever she started to worry that maybe they were getting too close, or, worse, that she was starting to depend on him for more than a BDSM education. Or that she was hoping blur those boundaries that had been so clear in the beginning—that would be both stupid and disastrous for her.

She hadn't expected an arrangement involving the exploration of sexual identity to be *simple*, exactly, but she was going to have to start being more careful. It was just too easy to feel comfortable around him, and to forget because of it.

She had all these thoughts on her mind, and then when she walked into his suite to use the shower—he'd seen how much she loved that giant shower, and he'd insisted she use it whenever she wanted; she wasn't too proud to turn *that* down—she'd seen the black bag. It was his gym bag.

In fact, she checked: yup, the gym bag.

Which, now that she thought about it, looked an awful lot like the bag he kept various BDSM toys in. In fact, it was the same stupid brand and model of black gym bag. Chance was the kind of guy who found one thing that worked for him, and then ordered as many of whatever it was as he needed. That man was lucky he was so good looking, because he didn't care about style at all.

But that still left the problem of the wrong bag.

Which was how, after worrying about getting entirely too involved with and attached to Chance Dalton, Lena ended up pulling on some jeans, got some quick info from Adra, and jogged down Abbot Kinney with the man's sweaty gym bag slung over her shoulder.

Lena was lucky; the gym was nearby. Billy's Boxing Gym. It looked like one of the only places on this stretch of the boulevard that hadn't been revamped by eager developers, just the original worn face, a hangdog sign, no lights outside. It looked like the place reeked permanently of male sweat. Like Chance's kind of place.

Still, she wasn't going to let him open his bag in front of his buddies and find a spreader bar if she could help it. She'd just feel bad if she did nothing just because she was having one of her freak-outs about boundaries or whatever. That was her issue, not his.

So she pushed open the old style shop door and stepped inside.

Whoa. Not air-conditioned. A gym. In L.A.. At the beginning of summer. Were these people all masochists?

Hard to tell. She could barely see in the dim light after the bright sunshine of the boulevard, but she heard the weird rhythm of many men pounding different bags, all at different times. There was some guy on the other side of the open space barking orders—in a ring?

She heard Chance's voice and turned—he was there, over in the corner, closer to the light, wearing these ridiculous mitts on his hands while a skinny little kid punched at him.

He was training a kid. She felt a smile start to spread across her face and tried to quash it.

"Hey, Chance," she said from a few feet away. He looked at her just as a bell went off and everyone stopped what they were doing. The sudden change was unnerving and made Lena feel like she was now an unwelcome center of attention, but she raised the bag off her shoulder so Chance could see it. "You forgot something."

The bell must have signaled a break. The kid who'd been punching at Chance turned around and looked at her.

And it was a terrible, terrible look.

A look of recognition.

Somehow the past two weeks of living in a Volare fantasy land where no one cared that half the country had seen photos of her naked and tied up, where no one mentioned the fact that Richie had since given a freaking *interview* about it, as though he hadn't had anything to do with it and was just a helpless victim, had allowed her to forget. She'd forgotten so much that she didn't think, for one second, that if she went into a boxing gym full of guys, some of them might recognize her.

And that one of the guys who recognized her might be a skinny teenager with freckles.

"Oh God," she whispered.

Chance didn't hesitate. "Mike, this is my friend Lena. Introduce yourself."

Chance nudged the kid, and Lena didn't miss the powerful glare he gave the boy. And she didn't miss the change in body language coming from Chance, either—shoulders hulking, brow heavy, like he had been when he'd come between her and Paul Cigna. He had moved next to her already, his sweat overpowering the stench of the gym, his scent somehow providing some sense of comfort.

It was sweet to see him being protective of her and paternal towards the kid at the same time. It gave her a brief feeling of optimism, a silver lining in this awful, awful situation.

"Mike," Chance said again.

Mike blinked, looked at Chance, and then tore at the Velcro on his glove with his teeth, slipped the glove off, and offered her his hand.

"Hi, Lena. I'm Michael," he said, and looked back at Chance. Chance tilted his head, like, *go on*. Michael gave her a shy smile and said, "I've heard you're a really good writer."

So this was surreal.

Lena was shaking a very sweaty, surprisingly small hand that belonged to a teenage boy whose voice hadn't even changed yet, and who, despite Chance's obvious efforts to manage the whole horrible situation, had obviously seen her naked. And tied up.

There were no rules of etiquette for a situation like this.

Lena just wanted to get the hell out of there. She had no idea how to deal with any of this; she somehow felt like she was doing something wrong just by *existing* in front of a child, and all of it was reminding her of how Richie had screwed up her life.

Finally she remembered her manners. "I don't know about really good, but thank you, Michael."

"No, really, Chance said you're one of the best he's ever read," he said, transparently eager to please.

Chance had said…wait, what?

Lena turned her head slowly to look at Chance. Another mindfuck. He'd read her work? When?

"Really," she said.

"Yeah, like, really good. Who'd you say she was like? Someone famous, right?" the boy asked, looking back up at Chance innocently.

Chance looked speechless for the first time

in her memory. He blinked, then shook it off. "Someone famous and dead, actually. Stop making her uncomfortable, Mikey."

"Ok, well, I just came by to bring your bag," she said, feeling the eyes of the entire gym on her. When was that bell going to ring again? "If you want I can take the other one back," she suggested.

"I don't have the other one," Chance said. "I'm just training Mike today, so I didn't need anything. And I'll walk back with you," he added, telling Mike, "Eight more rounds on the heavy bag, light conditioning today, and stop dropping that frigging shoulder. You're telegraphing every straight right. You got that?"

"Sure," Mike said. He waved at Lena, then struggled to get his glove back on while eying a giant digital clock attached to the bell. Apparently break was almost over.

Lena just wanted to disappear.

"Chance, you *really* don't have to—"

"Yes, I do. Don't argue. And give me that bag."

chapter 14

Chance decided to let Lena sort herself out after the incident at the gym. She had retreated, whether she knew it or not, into the guarded shell she'd only recently started to come out of. She was still holding things from him, but that was to be expected for someone with her issues. Chance wasn't too worried— she'd be ready eventually. Finding out that thirteen-year-old boys recognized you from BDSM photos that had been leaked online would be an unsettling experience for anyone, and he thought she'd actually handled that pretty well.

But the news that he'd read her work seemed to shake her up just as much. That, Chance decided, was weird. And his gut was still telling him that once she'd started to relax again, it was time to tackle that one.

Which was just as well. He had the public opening of Volare L.A. to plan for in the meantime. He and Roman had come up with the idea in the wake of the shitshow that was the publicity surrounding Roman and Lola's wedding; Chance figured if the public was going to be into it, why not give them somewhere to go? The Venice Beach location was perfect for that—Chance had just dedicated one building in the compound as the public club and had kept the rest separate. All the permits and such were in place, according to Ford, and all they had left to handle was the actual opening.

Chance took a hard line on the door policy. No idiots. Richie Kerns, for example, was already blacklisted.

That said, there were still all kinds of things to sort out, exactly the kinds of things that didn't interest him: guest list, promotional strategy, whatever. Good thing he had his ad hoc executive committee to deal with it. Adra had taken to it like a fish to water, and she didn't seem to mind working with Ford at all.

Chance knew he shouldn't complain. Many of the details of running the club didn't appeal to him, but it was a good job. His stake in Volare had made him financially independent, but hell, he needed something to occupy his time. And running Volare was way better than providing security for a company in some godforsaken warzone, given the kinds of trouble he'd gotten into in such places.

Or given the kind of trouble he'd gotten other people into in such godforsaken places.

Chance paused, his hand on the sliding glass door that led to the sun-drenched patio by the pool. Lena was out there. That was where he was going. Which meant he damn well needed to make sure he wasn't thinking about what had happened in Nigeria, or what had happened, years before that, to Jennie.

He'd been thinking about his past mistakes too often lately. Maybe because he couldn't help but wonder if he was making mistakes with Lena, too. The thought scared him.

But a man didn't run from stuff that scared him. He never had, never would. And neither did Lena, come to think of it. It was one of the things he admired in her.

He'd given her space. She'd settled down.

Now she was ready for what came next.

The glass door opened silently, a convenience that allowed him to sneak up on people intent on sunning themselves. Sometimes he couldn't resist.

Especially when it was Lena.

Holy… Just look at her. Lena. In a sky blue bikini, laying her beautiful body out, like the sun itself worshipped her. Wouldn't surprise him, come to think of it.

He walked over, took another good, long look at her just because, and sat down in the deck chair next to her. She had some sun tan lotion on the ground—coconut. That was what smelled so good. He took the bottle in one hand, and with the other reached across and unsnapped her top.

"That better be you," she said, eyes opening.

He grinned. "You know I can't resist 'em," he said. "Lie back."

He drizzled some lotion on her chest and indulged himself with rubbing it into her breasts, watching the soft flesh yield as her breathing changed and her nipples tightened into pert little buds.

"You're done avoiding me," he said.

He saw her smile playfully, eyes closed now against the sun. "Maybe."

"No, I'm telling you, you're done," he laughed, and tweaked a nipple.

She jerked upwards, her toned tummy flexing in the glare of the sun, and bit her lip to keep from smiling even more.

"Yes, sir," she said.

"That's better. Lay back."

She did, and now he just amused himself, fondling her breasts. He knew it would drive her crazy and it had been just too long. At least thirty-six hours, possibly forty-eight. Which, as far as he was concerned, was an eternity.

"I wasn't really avoiding you," she said

finally. "I mean, I was, but not on purpose. Not specifically. I was just avoiding…everything."

"I know," he said. "Did you figure out what you needed to figure out?"

She opened her eyes again, squinting at him, maybe trying to see what he knew. "I don't know," she said finally.

"You'll tell me when you do."

She laughed. "You probably won't give me a choice."

"Smart girl."

She stuck her tongue out. They settled back into an easy rhythm, Chance playing with her breasts, straying down her stomach, her hips, her thighs, and Lena trying to hide her increasing arousal. Let her try.

Finally she asked him, as he knew she would:

"When did you read my stuff?"

"When I packed it up. I didn't set out to, I was just trying to figure out what to bring. But I read the first page, and…" He shrugged. "I got hooked. I wouldn't have if I'd known you were so private about it, and haven't since. You'll let me know when you want me to. Unless, of course, I decide I need to for your training. Then you don't get a choice."

He detected a slight smile. She asked, "Which one?"

"It was untitled. Looked like you weren't done."

"Aw, crap. That's the one that needed *so* much work."

"Bull. It was amazing. I didn't finish, but I probably would have if you hadn't pulled that stunt with Paul Cigna."

At mention of the paparazzo's name he saw her flinch, almost imperceptibly, then try to cover it up. She was probably an excellent actress, with that degree of facial control, and with her expressiveness. That expressiveness had just told him Paul Cigna was very much still a real issue to her. She wasn't ready to tell him about that, either, possibly because she wasn't ready to be honest with herself about it — but she would be. And he was on it.

But right now, she deserved a little pampering. Especially considering what he had in store for her.

"Lift up," he said, patting her legs. He helped her lift them, then settled himself in between, resting her legs over his while he straddled the deck chair to face her. He had excellent access to everything this way.

He started on her thighs. He liked to see her muscles jump when he touched her, like his hands were electrified. This woman…

After a moment, she said, "You were really hooked?"

He looked up in surprise, not because of what she'd said, but because it was the first time he'd heard her sound shy.

"How can that surprise you?" he asked. "It's brilliant. I'm not a bookworm or anything, but I know a good story. Your agent should be all over that."

"Yeah, I tried that. Don't think he read it."

"His loss."

Her turn to shrug. Chance didn't like the expression that was gathering on her face, like a storm front moving in, threatening to ruin her mood.

"What about Adra?" he asked. "She's an agent now, right?"

He watched Lena very carefully. That suggestion hadn't dispersed the storm clouds—it had strengthened them. She looked somehow frightened, threatened. He wouldn't have that.

"Lena," he said sternly. "Tell me."

Lena pursed her lips, sighed, and opened her eyes. Every fleck of gold and green embedded in the rich brown of her irises lit up in the sun, dazzling him, locking him in place for the moment. They would have made it impossible to focus on anything else, if there'd been anything else he cared to focus on.

She said, "Look, Adra—and everyone else here—they all seem to like me. They *respect* me. I just really want to keep it that way."

"You assume that if they read your work they'd no longer respect you?"

No answer to that. Chance saw an

opportunity. He moved his hands lower on her belly and slid his thumbs under the edge of her bikini bottoms. She jumped a little. He wondered if *she* had noticed how much easier she found it to talk about things when she was physically exposed. He sure as hell had.

"Have you ever opened up?" he asked her.

She frowned, her brow furrowing and her eyes squinting open. She put her hand on top of his as if to stop him.

"What kind of question is that?" she said.

Chance just looked at the offending hand. Then at her. Awareness dawned on her, and she removed her hand.

"Not good enough," he said as he untied the double ties on the sides of her bikini bottoms. Lena's abs tightened, but she leaned back and said nothing. He picked up her wrists and placed them on the armrests of her deck chair, then tied them down with the ties from her now useless bottoms.

Not a strong restraint, but effective. Restrained, naked, and spread.

"You were saying something?" he said.

"You are a piece of work."

He spread her legs farther apart and watched her shudder.

"True. Answer the question."

"It's a bullshit question! Like, 'Have you ever given your heart to someone?' No, because that's some romantic nonsense. It doesn't work like that in the real world."

Chance let his hands roam aimlessly, rubbing her inner thighs, then her belly, then her breasts. Just teasing her.

"How does it work, then?" he asked lightly.

She opened her eyes and glared, even as he could smell her growing arousal. "Don't patronize me," she said. "It doesn't 'work' at all. People like each other for a time, or use each other, or get what they need, and move on."

"And what," he said, grazing his thumb over her clit, "do you think I'm getting from you?"

Lena flinched.

Chance studied her silently while he rubbed her stomach. She wasn't ready to tackle whatever lay behind this little display, either. He'd ease the tension out of her now, but it was pretty clear to him that, while what Richie Kerns had done to her was bad enough on its own, it had been made far worse because it tapped into an issue she already had. And he was already planning to deal with *that* himself.

But for now? He'd just tell her the truth.

"Everyone does like you and respect you," he said. "Hell, they're crazy about you. I doubt there's anything you could do that would change that at this point, kiddo. But you don't have to do anything you're not ready for."

She gave an audible sigh of relief and

wiggled her hips at him. He had her body ready to burst.

"Oh, don't get too comfortable," he laughed. "There's some other stuff I've decided that you *are* ready for."

She opened one eye. "Like what?"

"You'll see. Tonight. Eight o'clock. Be waiting for me on the north side of the hall around the atrium, top floor."

"That sounds…nefarious."

"It is."

"Why is it when you say something like that, I get turned on?"

"Didn't I tell you I'd train you good?" he said, slipping his thumbs between her inner and outer folds, searching for the bundle of nerves hidden there. Her tummy tightened again as he put pressure on her, the sensation almost visibly coiling up and down the length of her body, and her eyes flew open in surprise.

"What…what are you…?"

And then he just decided, *Aw, hell, I want to.*

He held her hips like a cup and bent down to drink.

He lapped at her slowly, in big teasing strokes, just glancing the sides of her clit, circling around it, driving her nuts until her thighs squeezed at the sides of his head and her hands reached for his head. He knew her body even better now, knew he could give her one quick orgasm to warm her up, even if he could have eaten her all day. He loved the taste of her.

They were so connected that he could feel her start to come in a way that drove him wild, like he could actually feel it *with* her, so that by the time he had her thighs shaking and her hips bucking, he was hard as steel and half there himself. She came silently, her body keening and her hands white-knuckled on the armrests, still afraid of being seen.

Chance eased her down, running his hands up and down her thighs, her stomach, her chest, while she gasped for air and jerked once or twice with aftershocks. He didn't know how she did it, but she always looked amazing after coming. While coming. All the time, really.

Too amazing to resist. He knew how far to push her. And he wanted to indulge himself. Just a preview of the way he'd take his pleasure, as a Dom, when she was through training.

"Lena," he said. "You back on Earth yet?"

"Yes, sir," she murmured.

"Good. Sit up."

He helped her scoot up the chair, raising the back of it for her, and got out from under her legs, standing over her while still straddling the chair. He blocked the sun now, so she could look at him without squinting.

He saw the idea occur to her, too. She licked

her lips.

"Suck me," he ordered.

She looked around a little nervously, still kind of spooked even though they were alone. She'd do this, and she'd be ready for tonight. And damn, did he want to see her suck him off.

Lena ran her hands up his legs, her eyes alight with something. She looked like she'd been waiting a while to do this, but there was still the nervousness, like she was worried she wouldn't do a good job. Her confidence had gotten better since she'd been at Volare, but if you looked you could still see the signs of the bruising she'd taken from Kerns.

By the time she got to his zipper, though, he could see she was thinking about one thing only. She was careful with his cock, which made him want to laugh; the damn thing could punch through two inches of steel at this point. Being around Lena all the time was giving it plenty of use.

She kissed the tip.

"Fuck," he said, as she licked away a drop of precum. Lena licked her way down the shaft, looking up at him with those eyes.

She was teasing him the way he teased her.

Oh, hell no.

Chance threaded his hand in her hair and watched her chest heave the way it did when he smacked her ass or put a finger inside her.

She liked the intimation of force. Then she looked up with those eyes again, smiling while she held his cock in her hands.

"Open," he growled.

She did, and he pushed in while she took his cock gladly, sucking slightly as he entered her mouth. He fisted her hair in his other hand and started to move in her mouth while she moaned. The site of her trying to take as much of his dick as she could was unbelievable, the look of lust in her eyes as she looked up at him maddening. She was so good, so, *so* good, and the found himself thrusting faster and faster, driven by the sounds she made and the way she reached for his balls, until he pushed her back against the back of the chair just as the rush hit the base of his dick.

"Swallow," he said.

She pulled back briefly, licking her lips, and smiled. Then she did.

All he could do was watch.

This woman…

He had plans for her already. But he added a few more orgasms to the list.

chapter 15

Lena tried to relax the rest of the afternoon, but she faced several obstacles: one, holy crap, what was Chance going to do to her later; two, she was still worked up about the questions he'd asked her; and three, she'd gotten another psychotic text message.

The text messages were starting to make less sense, honestly. Usually they commented on her and Chance, taunting her, asking when she was going to come out and get back in the scene—whatever the hell that meant. Maybe bars? Clubs? Trying to be seen in L.A.? She wasn't interested—but this one had just said, "You're delaying the inevitable."

Yeah, threatening.

She was starting to think she'd have to tell someone. And if she told anyone, she knew it had better be Chance. And that thought put her right back where she started, worrying about getting more involved, becoming dependent on the man, and making this arrangement into something it wasn't. And then, inevitably, getting hurt again.

She didn't like to admit how worked up she'd been by Chance's naked interrogation, but it had been obvious to both of them — she'd actually snapped at him. Come to think of it, she was surprised he'd just let that go.

Had she ever opened up to anyone? What did that even mean? And why had it hurt when *he* asked her? She knew why it hurt, generally, but she thought she'd grown a thicker skin under most circumstances. In private, it hurt because she wanted to be able to do that, and *that* made her feel stupid, because Lena Simone Maddox knew better than that, and had since she was a child. Even now she'd watch a sappy movie and part of her would want to rail at the screen: *That's not real! Real life doesn't work out like that!*

She'd learned that the hard way the first time her mother had kicked her out for one of her mom's boyfriends. Then she'd learned it again the second time. And so on. But the worst part was that by the time she got to L.A., sixteen but looking twenty and lying about her age, she *still* hadn't been smart enough: she'd gotten taken for rent money by the first guy she'd gotten involved with. Had she opened up to him? Was that the problem?

Over the years it had just been a slow process of acclimation. She was proud of the fact that she'd gotten tougher, tough enough to mostly avoid getting her heart broken— because, in fact, she'd realized Richie *hadn't* broken her heart, because she'd never given it to him.

Of course, she hadn't gotten smart enough or tough enough to avoid getting exploited. So there was that.

It was the one thing that Chance Dalton hadn't seemed to understand right away, and that made her feel uneasy. Like he didn't get it because he'd been lucky in his own life. The privileged romanticism of people who got lucky.

Wait, wait, wait — that's not fair, she thought. She was just being bitter and angry. She didn't know jack about Chance's life, except that something had screwed him up, too.

And that he'd read her script.

And that he thought she was brilliant.

Lena smiled. Maybe it wasn't smart to open up heedlessly, and maybe she had some things to resolve, but she could let herself bask in that particular revelation for a while. She could trust the man with her body and with her work. Maybe that was enough.

By the time eight o'clock rolled around, she was in a frenzy of anticipation.

She'd actually wondered about what to wear.

Then she realized whatever she wore was probably just going to come right off. That did *not* help.

Eight o'clock found her in a light wrap dress and sandals, her hair tied back in a loose knot, climbing the floating stairs to the top floor of the main building, looking down at the atrium below. She'd walked through it on her way to the stairs and had felt comforted to see a bunch of familiar faces — Ford was there, and Adra, giving Ford some perplexing looks, and Declan Donovan, the rock star who last week had insisted that she try a bite of his first attempt at baking, part of some sort of stupid competition he'd had with Adra. Once Lena got over the surrealism of the moment, she'd agreed to taste test his attempt. Lena *thought* he'd meant to make cookies, but the results had been…something else. The guy had been a sweetheart. And apparently he was also a Dom. Some sub was going to be very lucky.

Look at her, using words like Dom and sub and feeling like she knew what she was talking about. This place…this place was already to feel like home. Sort of.

She could see them all from the railing on the top floor, right below, still sitting around and chatting after their meeting. The acoustics in the atrium were pretty good. She could almost understand what they were saying.

It almost distracted her from thoughts of Chance and what he had planned for her. Almost, but not quite. Probably nothing could have done that.

"Look at you," he said from behind her.

She turned, leaning back against the railing, and just enjoyed the way he looked at her. The man knew how to make a woman feel good in more ways than one. He was dressed like he always was, in that effortless dressed-down cool of a real life movie star or a country singer or something. It was just that body, and that impish grin, and the square jaw, and the buzzed head. All of it, really. Irresistible.

"I'm here," she said.

"Yes you are," Chance said, coming closer. He toyed with the tie that held her dress together, tugging on it to see what kind of give it had. "This all it takes?"

Lena breathed a little faster. "Yes."

He flashed that smile. "This is a good dress."

Oh jeez. She felt her legs quivering already. And the suspense was just killing her. He didn't tear off her dress, though now that was practically all she could think about; he didn't tell her what he was going to do—he didn't do *anything*. Just drove her insane.

"Is there something I'm supposed to do?" she asked. She hated that she sounded so nervous. That had been happening a lot.

He gave her a playful frown, then bent down and bit her neck. She made a sound in shock, a kind of cut-off squeak, but he just held her there, his teeth gripping her neck, his hand at her waist, until she relaxed into him.

Oh God, he *owned* her.

"That's better," he said, lifting his head to look down at her with those bright eyes. "You're gonna need to relax, sweetheart."

She nodded, not trusting herself to form words just yet. He'd *bitten* her...

"So tell me something," he said, leaning on the railing and looking down as she turned to face him. "Why is it that you, who is so ordinarily brave, seem so hung up on what other people think of you?"

"Ordinarily brave?" she asked.

He smiled. "That was unclear, huh? I meant that it's your ordinary state, not that it's a common thing. It's *un*common. See? You're a writer, I'm not."

She felt her cheeks get hot. Of all the things this man had said to her, of all the things he'd *done* to her, that was what got her. Yeah, that made sense.

But he was talking nonsense again. It bugged her the same way it had that afternoon.

"Don't pretend like it doesn't matter what

people think of you," she said quietly, turning to look down at the people gathered below. "I know people like to say that, but it's just…wrong. Your professional prospects damn well change based off of what people think of you."

"I'm not saying it doesn't matter, or that it should or it shouldn't," he said. "I'm saying I think you assume that people will think bad things about you, and that just astounds me."

She frowned. "That's not—"

"You don't trust the world to treat you right, Lena," he said. "And maybe it hasn't in the past. But that's not now. Here, it's different. You have to learn there are places in the world where you'll be cherished for what you are."

She was stunned. His words, what he'd said—she'd thought he hadn't understood. But he had. He'd understood perfectly.

Lena looked at him with the beginnings of tears in her eyes, which is how she missed it when he slipped one soft leather cuff over her right wrist and attached it to the railing.

She looked down as he reached over and cuffed the left wrist and did the same thing.

"Oh, you're kidding," she said.

"I don't ever joke about this," he laughed. "Except when I do, of course."

She was starting to get that tingling feeling all over, that rush that said it was starting. Lena couldn't help but look down, where that crowd of familiar faces was still gathered, all of them lounging comfortably on the plush chairs and sofas. None of them expecting to see her get fucked several stories above.

Or maybe they were.

She flushed with heat and tested the cuffs. No, she wasn't going anywhere. And those were Chance's hands running down the sides of her body.

"Put your hands on the railing and step back, sweetheart," he said. "Bend at the waist and lean into it like you might have to be there for a while."

Well, *that* was suggestive.

So she was afraid. Yes. She was, in fact, kind of shaking as she gripped the railing and bent over to lean into it, putting some of her weight on her arms. There was no way to hide the shaking in her bare, treacherous arms, and Chance took a moment to stop whatever he was doing behind her to run his big, warm hands down the length of her arms, up and down, murmuring into her ear the whole time.

She stopped shaking.

She didn't know exactly what he was going to do, but she knew enough to be freaked out. She knew it would be in full view of those people down there. She knew it would force her to face that. And while there was that rotten, familiar tightness in her chest and her adrenaline was pumping and everything was telling her to run, she knew she could do this. With Chance standing behind her, she could do it. Giving up control to him was the only thing that had felt consistently right, that had freed her when she'd felt most trapped, that allowed her to just...*feel*.

She trusted him.

"Good girl," he whispered.

Then he spread her legs. She closed her eyes and felt a cuff go around one ankle, then the other, and saw him attach the tethers to different parts of the railing.

Her legs were staying spread.

Chance let his finger tips dance up the inside of one leg until he reached her sex, bare, the way she knew he'd want it. He swiped his finger down the length of her slit, saying, "Good thinking."

She clenched, and he laughed.

"You are so much fun, you know that?" he said, whispering into her ear again.

"Don't tease me," she said, wavering.

"I'm not teasing you, Lena," he said. "You're gonna have to get used to the idea that I like being around you, is all."

She felt his hand on the back of her neck, holding her delicately, then rubbing her bare back down to her waist, her hips.

"You're gonna have to get used to the idea that I think you're fucking amazing," he said. "In bed and out."

Lena felt a tug at her waist — the tie that held the wrap dress closed, and *on*. He was slowly — oh God, so slowly — pulling it loose.

She closed her eyes.

"Actually, sweetheart, you should probably get used to the idea that a whole lot of people think you're amazing, whether you know it or not," he said as the tie pulled free. "And I'm taking about Lena, not Simone Maddox."

Chance was silent as he let the dress slip off her in its own time, the material whispering against her skin as it slid, so slowly it was like another caress.

"But that," he said softly, "is neither here nor there, at the moment. God. Damn."

Lena still hadn't opened her eyes, but Chance's talk about her naked body would get her every time. She smiled, even as she started to shake again, her arms rattling the cuff clasps on the railing.

"Shhh," he said, and then his warm hands were on her bare skin again, and the sensation of his touch overwhelmed everything else. Her mind followed him as he trailed down her back, across her stomach, her chest. While he held her breasts, kissed her neck, ran his hands over her hips and down her legs.

"Open your eyes, Lena," he said finally.

Lena took a deep breath and obeyed. Her eyes swung around wildly, taking it all in. They were alone on this floor, at least on the outer hall landing, but Ford and Declan were still there, two stories below, still oblivious, but for how long? And she knew there were others around.

"It occurred to me," Chance said from behind her, while one hand snaked in under her to play with her nipple, "that I'm really the only one who knows how incredible you look when you come. That doesn't seem fair."

Lena muffled a laugh. He was making her feel a little crazy. She was cuffed to a railing, her legs spread, naked, and he was…what was he even doing? Was she dreaming?

"You're trying to drive me crazy, right?" she said.

"Only a little bit," he said lightly. "But that's about to change."

Smack.

He'd spanked her. Hard enough to bring stinging tears to her eyes, hard enough for the pain to sizzle into pleasure as it traveled through her body, hard enough for the slap of his hand on her ass to be heard everywhere.

Smack.

Smack. Smack. Smack.

Her breasts swung forward with every blow, and the swelling between her legs grew painfully. There wasn't any more room for thinking. No more room for why she wanted this, for why it felt so good, even while it hurt, even while it humiliated her, why it still felt so *right.*

"Lena, what did you do wrong?" Chance asked.

That voice. Still warm and safe, yet *hard.* Commanding. She opened her mouth, shook her head.

Smack.

"C'mon, sweetheart," he said. "You know."

"I avoided you," she gasped. "I should have told you what...what was going on. Why I was upset."

"Good," he said, sweeping his hand across her stinging ass. "Only four more to go for that. You're almost there."

Smack. She whimpered, already feeling sore. Was he really —?

Smack. Smack. Smack.

On the last one she cried out, sure her ass must be glowing, and unsure what to do with the feelings that swirled wildly within her. There was nothing *to* do, except ride them and remain receptive. Chance had made sure of that.

He said, "I can't look out for you, Lena, I can't take care of you, and I can't give you what you need, if I don't know what's going on. That is *dangerous.* I am going to tie you up and do unspeakable things to you and I need to know that it's going to work for you."

She laughed, half laugh, half sob, her body a confusing jumble of emotions and sensations, the throbbing in her pussy louder than all the others combined.

"Unspeakable things?" she asked.

He thrust a finger into her, deep. "Starting now," he said.

chapter 16

She moaned; and his finger inside her, penetrating her, felt even better when she heard him laugh and slap her thigh. A rush of affection ran through her when she realized he had avoided her raw and sensitive butt.

"Bend over with those beautiful breasts on the railing," he said. "Give 'em a good view."

Lena balked. Declan and Ford and Adra and whoever else…

What would they think of her?

"But—"

"Do you trust me?" Chance asked.

"Yes," she said. That—*that* she was sure of. And she always had her safeword.

"Good, 'cause I'm not giving you a choice."

With one hand holding her between her legs and his finger still inside her, he started to push her forward while his other hand pushed down on her back. He really wasn't kidding. She was doing this.

"Ok," she panted. "Ok!"

"All right, then."

Awkwardly, with her legs still cuffed and spread apart, she shuffled toward the railing. She had a little more slack on her legs the closer she got to the railing, but not much. She took a deep breath, reminded herself that Chance was always behind her, and bent over so her breasts were pushed up and visible.

"Good girl," Chance said. "Now, how much noise you're going to make is up to you. But I'm betting I can get you to go pretty loud."

"You jerk," she muttered.

He smacked her lightly right on her pussy, and she cried out. Not only was that the shock of a lifetime, but holy crap, it felt good.

"See?" he said. "And keep talking like that if you want to get spanked so hard you can't sit down. I'm not kidding."

"Fine."

"What's that?"

"I meant 'yes, sir,'" she said quickly. "Sorry."

He kept his hand on her, but bent down to whisper in her ear, his free hand straying to her breasts again. "You are going to be one fine sub, Lena."

Going to be?

Going to be?

She was chained, naked, to a railing, in front of a bunch of different guys, all because he'd ordered it! *Going*—

Cold gel fell into the crack of her ass and immediately silenced her righteous indignation. She shivered, and she was pretty sure she puckered, too, all of it involuntarily.

First there was a finger, moving in tiny little circles around her anus, hitting nerves she'd never knew existed. Anal sex wasn't something she'd given much of a try. She hadn't really trusted anyone with a part of her she knew could be easily damaged.

In retrospect, maybe that was a sign that she shouldn't have trusted those guys with anything at all.

Chance's finger, though, Chance's finger...so delicate, his touch, and yet firm. Every time he broached the tight ring it felt like a whole new kind of intrusion, and sent bolts of sensation shooting directly to her clit.

"Relax, sweetheart," he said. "This isn't too big. You can do this."

This?

Then she felt it. More lube, and then hard plastic. He said it wasn't too big, but still it felt impossibly large, going the wrong direction...

"Bear down on it, Lena," Chance said, his voice calm and controlled. Soothing. "Go on, you can do it."

She closed her eyes and did what he said, and he pushed it into her with a little *pop* she could feel.

It felt huge.

It flared against her cheeks, cold and unyielding, and the constant sense of "holy crap, that shouldn't be there" just reinforced how much she was simply *his*. To play with, to fuck, to do with as he wished, even if that seemed to mostly consist of coming up with unexpected ways to make her feel good.

"How are you doing?" he asked, stroking her back.

She nodded, trying to come up with words. "Good," she said. "It's…it's good."

His laughter was soft, subtle this time. "Thought it might be. You might even be able to take me now," he said, and she moaned at the thought. "But not yet. Your eyes better still be open. They looking up yet?"

Lena's eyes had been open, but she'd only been obeying the letter of the law, not so much the spirit. She'd been staring resolutely at a blank spot in the wall across the atrium, on the other side of the building. Not down.

Not down.

"Lena," he said, a warning in his tone.

"Shit," she muttered.

You can do this. His hand on her back helped. She looked down.

They weren't looking up. They weren't

looking up!

"Well?"

"No," she said, and later, when she'd think back on it, she would realize that she'd sounded too happy about it.

"We'll have to do something about that," he said.

Something moved the plug. His palm, as his fingers drifted lower, towards her entrance, his palm leaned on the plug, moving it in circles, raking across those nerves, making it feel…so much bigger. Huge. Impossible. *Filling* her.

She started to moan.

"I'm going to take this ass one day," he said. "Soon. Spread more for me. And keep those eyes open and looking down."

He was going to make her scream. She could tell already. He was going to make her scream, and then everybody would know what was going on and where to look and there was nothing she could do about it. It was inevitable, so why did it still hold dread for her? Why —?

Something started to buzz. She knew she wasn't allowed to move, couldn't look back, but holy crap, did it sound big.

And then he touched it to the base of the plug.

"Oh my *God*," she moaned, loudly.

It was vibrating inside her, sparking inside her, and each vibration echoed in her body as her legs, her arms, her stomach started to shake. She tried to speak, and it came out as a wail.

Then Chance plunged ruthlessly into her vagina.

He didn't prepare her, didn't start slow, and the sudden stretch of her flesh pinched painfully even as she screamed out in pleasure.

Now she screamed.

She'd never, ever felt so full. So taken. As sudden as his intrusion had been, now all she wanted was for him to *move*. She was so close, perpetually high on the vibrations in her anus, the feeling of fullness, the knowledge now, the freaking *sight*, of Ford and Declan and people she didn't even know looking up at her getting taken from behind by Chance Dalton.

How did he know?

How did he know this would be…?

Slowly, achingly slowly, he started to pull out of her. She whined, he laughed. He pressed the vibrator down harder as he slid back into her, and her eyes rolled back in her head. She didn't know how much longer she could stand it if he just kept torturing her, stringing her higher and higher while her body tensed and coiled around him, desperate for release.

She had her answer as the vibrations ceased, an arm came around her waist, and he pushed deeper inside her.

"Now you come screaming," he said in her

ear.

And as he started to move, thrusting violently inside her, pounding her relentlessly, the round head of the vibrator touched her clit, and she did exactly as she was told.

~ * ~ * ~

Chance was pretty sure that Lena had passed out, temporarily, when she came up against the third floor railing. Her legs had buckled, and she would have collapsed if he hadn't caught her. He'd come yelling her name as she contracted around him, but her orgasm had just gone on, and on, and on. He didn't know how women did it. He was pretty sure something like that would have killed him.

But he'd caught her, and he'd carefully removed the restraints and then the plug, and then he'd held her in his arms as he carried her back to his room. She wasn't coherent until they'd been sitting in his monster green chair for untold minutes, just breathing together, Chance placing light kisses on her head. He couldn't resist touching her. As soft as she was, there was something magnetic about her.

But when she did finally come to, all she said was one thing.

"Thank you."

chapter 17

Lena drifted down to Earth from the heights of subspace, or her orgasm, or both, at a leisurely, lazy pace. She had that luxury, because Chance was taking care of her. As always.

He'd held her until she was somewhat functional, and then carried her back to her own room, where he held her again until she fell asleep. This was the major barrier she'd set up, and he hadn't questioned it yet, though some nights she passed out in his bed after being fucked senseless; if she made a conscious choice, it was to sleep in her own space. He respected it, which she was grateful for, but she also wondered if there was a time limit on his patience with that. Or, rather, on his patience for her lack of explanation. But her ability, her choice, to retreat into her own space was the thing that comforted her when she really began to fear that she was coming to depend on Chance.

So it was that he asked her if she wanted to go to sleep, and where, and then he carried her there and stayed with her until she was out.

Waking up in the dark without him there was, for the first time, jarring.

And then she couldn't get back to sleep.

There were a couple of things that kept her awake, but chief among them, besides the ever-present, gnawing anxiety that she was getting in way over her head with this man, was the fact that she still hadn't told him about the harassment from Paul Cigna.

Or whoever was sending her those texts.

Her ass was still a little sore from the spanking he'd given her. From a *spanking*. She probably wasn't going to get over that anytime soon, but the fact remained that his essential point had been correct: he did need to know about things that affected her, psychologically and physically. If she was going to ask him to do this for her, to train her as her Dom, she had to give him the tools he needed to do it safely.

She'd been an idiot.

She couldn't help but wonder if that idiocy was more about her own issues than anything else. Well, no, of course it was. It always was. That didn't make it any less difficult to overcome.

And that scene! What he'd done for her with that alone…she didn't have words. And she knew it wasn't over. She knew the next part would come when he forced her to face all those people and see that they still accepted her.

Damn brilliant man.

Her gratitude for that only heightened the guilt she felt for keeping the texts from him. She didn't want to go wake him up, but she didn't think she'd be able to sleep until she got this off her chest, even if she dreaded that it would become a big deal.

She decided to take a shower instead.

He'd given her a room adjoining his own suite, with a door to his master bathroom. She had her own, but he made a point of telling her to use the shower whenever she felt like it. He was a heavy sleeper and generally kind of oblivious unless he was doing his Dom thing, and he'd insisted it wouldn't bother him, no matter what time of night.

Well, he hadn't lied to her yet.

Her eyes had long since adjusted to the dark, and she'd always been a fan of dark, hot showers. She had just located her towels when she thought she heard something from Chance's bedroom.

Or was she imagining it? Just for an excuse?

She was standing buck-naked in the man's bathroom, trying to eavesdrop on him while he was sleeping. That didn't speak highly to sanity. There was every possibility that she was imagining things.

Nope, there it was again. A kind of groan, a rustle. Not the fun kind, either, though it occurred to her, as she opened the door to his room, that he had every right to sleep with other women. He had the right; they hadn't talked about it, but it would crush her.

There wasn't any other woman. Just Chance, writhing in his bed, covered in sweat. His face was screwed up in pain. Distress.

For a moment she stood there, shocked.

Then she went to him.

She knew that on some level maybe she should be scared. A man of his size and strength, a military vet, a guy who'd done security work in probably terrible places, having an obviously violent nightmare—there were a number of things to be scared of. But she wasn't. Maybe that was stupid, but this was the man who took care of her so diligently, who put so much thought into her welfare that he orchestrated insane scenes, who'd made her feel better about herself than she ever had before.

"Chance," she whispered. She didn't know what to do. If she touched him while he was asleep, he might flip out. But he was so obviously in pain, his fists clenched at his sides, his arms corded with straining muscle, the tattoos on them distorted as he fought some imaginary enemy.

"Chance," she said again, hoping against hope that he would just wake up.

He sat bolt upright, eyes wide and roving around the room. His chest heaved, dripping with sweat, while he rapidly checked all entrances and exits. Assessed any threats.

He blinked.

He looked at her.

He was still breathing hard when he reached out for her hand, enfolding it in his so that it seemed to disappear. The pad of his thumb rasped over the delicate skin of her wrist as his body calmed down, retreating slowly from the red alert state of whatever terrible thing he'd been dreaming about.

With her other hand she touched his shoulder, lightly.

Chance didn't say anything. He only lay back down, slowly, pulling her down with him. Gathering her to him like something precious. He turned onto his side and held her close to his chest, big arms wrapped around her, sheltering her from any threat, real or imagined, and threw one leg over her body.

A bomb could go off and she'd be fine.

Lena fell asleep to the thudding of his powerful heart, thinking that maybe she could finally give him something, too.

The next morning, Chance was gone.

Lena frowned, her hands searching the bed covers like she might find him under there. That…was not like him. At all. He'd left a note saying he had to go deal with some sort of permit or zoning fiasco, which she didn't doubt, but she'd become so accustomed to his considerate style that she almost expected him to, like, wake her up with a kiss, first.

Ok, no, that's ridiculous, she thought.

Still, though. The point was that it was a change, not that it was unreasonable.

Well, ok. Ok. She could navigate this. She was so used to guarding herself from becoming dependent on Chance that she had given little if any thought to the possibility that he might grow close to her. But wasn't that exactly what he'd said he couldn't do?

And how was she going to tell him about the texts *now*?

"Crap," she said out loud.

There was nothing to do but make breakfast and mull it over.

Lena couldn't help but wonder what Volare L.A. would be like once it expanded. It was still small, still just a core group of people, while they set up the public club and carefully searched for new members. For this short period of time, though, it felt like a small family in a giant, well appointed house. Kind of nice, really.

Lena loved the downstairs kitchen the best. She didn't know how the New York club was set up, but she gathered it was more sort of formal? This place had a very California sense of openness that she loved. Plus giant slate countertops, every appliance she'd ever seen, and some she hadn't. She'd identified one: a *sous vide* cooker. She'd guessed they were eventually going to hire a chef. Or at least someone who knew what *sous vide* was.

But for now? It was the most overly equipped omelet and cookie factory in the hemisphere.

She padded down there in one of Chance's shirts and her favorite sweats, bleary-eyed and yawning, and totally unprepared for the redheaded hurricane she found raiding the fridge. All the fridges, actually. And apparently the tall redhead had gotten to the cabinets, too.

"Um, hello?" Lena said.

"You must be Lena," the redhead said over her shoulder. "Look, I'm not going to get into it, but this is very important: where the hell is the chocolate?"

Maybe Lena's brain wasn't working properly yet. She blinked and turned the words over in her head. No, the woman was definitely hunting for emergency chocolate.

"I don't think there is any."

The woman turned with such slow,

exaggerated horror that Lena giggled. She was beautiful, almost stunning, really, and also about to kill someone for some chocolate. Lena wanted to be helpful.

"Declan used the only chocolate I know of to make his, um, cookies, I guess you'd call them?"

"*Where?*"

"If no one threw them out, they're probably under that cover, right there. But look, I *really* wouldn't—"

"Oh, Lena," the woman said, tossing the covering aside to get to the plate of chocolate-containing abominations, "You seem nice, and I want you to like me, so please, please don't make me act any crazier than I already am. It's already kind of an adjustment."

"Ok, well, before you actually take a bite and hate me forever, who are you?"

The woman smiled at her, a brilliant smile, just *glowing.* "I'm Lola," she said.

Lola Theroux!

Chance's cousin! The woman who ran Volare New York, who had just gotten married to Roman Casta, who—

"Holy shit, you're pregnant, aren't you?" Lena blurted out.

Lola spit out her "cookie," which was really just as well, considering.

"How...?" she asked, looking genuinely shocked.

"I don't know, it just…I mean, the chocolate hunt, and you look amazing, frankly, like your skin. You could be in commercials. And you were feeling crazy. I just kind of guessed—I wasn't even serious. And I, um, spoke without thinking. And…now I know. Sorry about that."

Lola ran a hand through her red hair, clearly freaking out.

"You can't tell anyone. *Nobody* knows. I barely know. I did the test when I got off the plane. That is just…"

"I really am sorry." Lena cringed.

"Well, we're certainly friends now, aren't we?" Lola said, leaning back on the counter.

Then she took another bite of cookie.

And swallowed it.

"Honestly, if you don't want anyone else to know yet, you should probably stop eating those cookies," Lena said.

Lola snorted. "They're so bad, but I just can't stop. What are they made out of, baking soda?"

"And salt, I think."

"Oh God, throw them out," Lola laughed, pushing the plate away from her. "I can't be trusted with them. That is so gross."

Lena laughed again, delighted to have this bond of deadly cookies with Lola Theroux, and realized she was absurdly happy to have met this woman at all. No, she was absurdly happy to be friends with this woman. She was happy that Lola wanted Lena to like *her*.

"So, um, you've heard about me?" Lena asked.

"Ah," Lola said, wiping the last remaining horrible crumbs from her mouth. "Oh yes, you are the woman who's managed to get Chance to be her Dom for more than a week at a time. Yeah, I've heard about you."

"It was kind of a special circumstance. He's doing it to help me get over something."

"Your douchebag ex-boyfriend and his shenanigans?"

"Bingo."

For the first time, the fact that someone knew about it all didn't make Lena cringe. It was a relief, the way Lola talked about it like something matter-of-fact, like it wasn't the end of the world, just something crappy that had to be endured.

"Well, that is just like Chance," Lola said, smiling. "He can't tear himself away from a woman in trouble. But don't think that means it wasn't about you," she added. "You're not the first woman in trouble to come his way, not by a long shot. He usually doesn't get so personally involved."

Lena did not know how to respond to this. She didn't even know how to feel about it. She was both relieved and horrified at the idea that she might be just another damsel in distress for Chance to help; she was also both relieved and horrified that she might *not* be just another damsel in distress, that she might be special in some way, something that meant this was getting more complicated than she could handle.

Well, after last night, wasn't it already complicated?

Lena was a mess.

"I need your advice," she said to Lola.

"Well, that was quick." Lola giggled. "Oh, wow, ignore me. I'm sorry, these hormones are just...I'm probably going to cry again in, like, five minutes. Just ignore it. Ask away, I promise my brain is working fine."

"You're one of the lucky ones that gets to have fun with all this pregnancy stuff, aren't you?"

"Shh," Lola admonished. "Don't use the p-word. Just tell people I'm eccentric or something. Now c'mon, ask away."

"You know you're the reason Chance helped me? With the whole paparazzo thing?"

"You think I'm the reason he helped you? No, honey, Chance does what he wants, trust me. And that wasn't your question."

Lena sighed. Lola was obviously just as stubborn as Chance. And Lena had heard she was a switch, someone who could be both dominant and submissive. She could believe it — there was something in the tone of that last sentence...

"What's wrong with Chance?" Lena asked.

Lola grew quiet, and Lena could feel the other woman studying her. Like she was evaluating whether she could trust her.

Again, like Chance.

"What happened, specifically?" Lola asked.

"Nothing bad. I mean, he didn't hurt me or lose control or anything like that. God, he would never—"

"I know what you mean. Go on."

"He was really clear that he won't get into relationships because he's fucked up in some way, which, I'm fine with that, honestly. I get it. But last night he had some kind of nightmare. I say it like that and it sounds stupid, but trust me, if you'd seen him…"

"He's been different since he got back," Lola said quietly. "I've been worried about him. Something he was holding back, something I know is hurting him. He hasn't talked to Roman or me about it, but I think something happened on his last security job. And the only other time I've seen him like this…"

Lola trailed off. Lena could see that she'd asked about something raw, something real, and now that Lena knew there really was something there, she didn't know what to do. She knew what she felt, but she didn't know what the rules were, whether she could push Chance, whether she *should*.

"When else have you seen him like that?"

she asked.

Lola sighed. "I know this is horrible to do to you, but this is something that Chance really needs to tell you himself. And you need to talk to him about it, because he's your Dom. And believe me when I tell you that *I'm* going to talk to him about it, because that is how we roll at Volare. Lots of redundancies in taking care of each other."

"Oh, please don't," Lena said. "I should have asked him about it first, and now — "

"Don't worry about it. He'll expect me to be concerned. He would do the same for me if I had something going on and I was training a sub. If he screwed up with you, even a little bit, it would probably damage him more than it would you."

Weirdly, even though Lena was the one getting tied up and spanked, she could believe this. Chance would never forgive himself if anything ever happened to her.

And she was grateful for the opportunity to spill all of this to someone who would actually understand. Lena let it all just rush out of her. "I don't know how to talk to him without crossing a line. I don't know if that makes any sense to anyone else, but he was so clear about not getting into a relationship, and *I* was so clear about it, and I really am totally fine with it, and I just…don't. I really don't want to cross a line I shouldn't."

"Uh huh," Lola said, smiling a little too knowingly for Lena's liking. "You are fine with it, and you don't want to. You've said that a few times. Well, listen, in my experience these things tend to work themselves out. Sometimes it can take *way* too long, if someone happens to be particularly stubborn," she added darkly, "but, you know, it does happen eventually. Just do what you think is right, Lena."

"You seem confident."

"Yup. And now I'm going to cry. For literally just…no reason. Crying. Here it comes."

Lena stifled a laugh, even as she was getting some tissues. "You know, I don't know how long you're going to be able to keep this a secret," she said.

"I know," Lola sobbed. "But it's just that Ford says Chance has been so happy lately, and you're all worried, and, I just…oh *God*, seriously just ignore me. I should not be talking right now. At all. To anyone."

"Would it be terrible if I used this to my advantage and got you to spill?"

"Yes!"

"Ok," Lena giggled, handing Lola another tissue. "I'm sorry, I'll be good, I promise."

"Hey," came a voice from the door to the terrace. "What's wrong?"

Chance stood there, holding a take out bag from the breakfast burrito place he'd seen Lena frequent every day since he'd moved in, looking like he didn't know who to be more worried   about.

chapter 18

Chance was bewildered. First, there was the fact that Lola was here, in L.A., which he was thrilled about. Except that she was crying. And talking to Lena. Who was…laughing?

And now they were whispering together?

"Lena," he said, going full Dom voice right away. "Talk to me."

"Don't pull that, Chance," Lola said. "I give her amnesty, she's talking to me about *my* problems, and she's wonderful. Also, I'm just hormonal, ignore it. Now get over here and give me a hug."

Great, Lola with PMS. He had no idea how women managed it, but they did, something he was eternally grateful for. If he had to deal with random hormones and the rest he'd lose his mind.

Chance moved in on Lola with his arms wide open and he caught Lena snickering as he swept his cousin up in a great big bear hug. His sub would pay for that later.

Just as soon as he could get the image of her standing over him, worried, caring about him, touching him, out of his head. Just as soon as he could forget how good it had felt to hold her through the night.

Right. Just like that.

Probably he had some things to take care of before he involved her in another scene. He was now doubly glad that Lola was here. He could use some decent advice. He'd avoided imposing his problems on Lola and Roman, as they were figuring their own relationship out, not wanting to get in the way of those two dumb kids finally realized that they were madly in love with each other, but maybe now it was time.

The last thing he expected was to get blindsided by his little sub first.

"Chance," Lena said. "Can we talk?"

"Go," Lola said, waving him away. "We have all week, and I want to poke around anyway. And send someone to go buy pickles. Do you know you have zero pickles? Oh, damn. Don't listen to me, just…go."

Chance wasn't even listening to his cousin. One of the first things he'd learned as a Dom was that one's authority was only as strong as it was fair. And Chance knew in his heart that he needed to care for Lena after what she'd seen the night before.

So it wasn't like he had a choice.

But every dominant fiber of his being bridled and demanded that he take note and establish the proper order of the world later. Principally, Lena under him, trussed and tied.

But right now, they could talk.

Chance had tried to sort through the way he felt about what had happened the previous night. It had been a nightmare, obviously, one of those terrifying collages of every shitty thing he'd ever seen or felt or feared. So of course it didn't make sense. It had started back in Nigeria, when he'd learned the Asala family was missing, and then he'd suddenly been back home, watching Jennie get beaten to a bloody pulp and unable to do anything about it. He'd been frozen in place, unable to move, something he recognized now as sleep paralysis, but in the dream it hadn't mattered. He was just failing to protect her all over again.

And then he was at Jennie's funeral, something he hadn't been to in real life, when everybody started pointing. Screaming. This time, he was the monster.

Yeah, that had sucked.

And then he'd woken up, terrified he'd find himself somehow like *them*, the men he'd beaten up or held down before they killed someone, just as bad, really a monster. And she was there. Looking at him like she cared. Like she was worried.

It had made all the difference.

Holding her, knowing he had her safe, had made all the damn difference. It was the same way she'd calmed him, only magnified, multiplied. She made him feel human.

How the hell was he supposed to explain any of that?

"What happened last night, Chance?" Lena asked quietly.

"No foreplay?" he said. "You've got a lot to learn about leading, sweetheart."

"Don't do that," she said. "If I can't avoid stuff, you shouldn't do it, either."

He smiled at her. She had a point. He could be proud of her and irritated at the same time.

"I'm not avoiding anything. But don't forget who I am, either."

Chance strolled over to the waist-height wall around the edge of the roof garden. Lena had led him up here to talk, something he privately appreciated. It was a good space for her now, somewhere she felt comfortable, safe. He felt good about that.

"Yeah, ok," he said, sweeping a palm across the fuzz on his head. Almost time to buzz it again. "I haven't exactly worked all this out yet to my own satisfaction, but you are involved now, aren't you? The short version?"

"Any version," she said.

He filled his lungs and let it out slowly. Fine.

"So my last security job was on a pipeline in Nigeria," he said. "There are bands of...well, bandits, I guess. The oil companies call them terrorists, but they're just gangs with guns who want money and think they can do whatever the hell they want. Anyway, I became friendly with this family in one of the out-of-the-way villages. It was because of the kid — he used to play soccer with me. I got him an actual ball and everything, though, looking back, that might have drawn attention to them. Anyway, near the end of my contract I got into it with some of these gangs, these bad guys."

Chance looked at her, tried to gauge her reaction. Her eyes were big, open hazel pools. Well, he had to tell her.

"The Asalas went missing. Gone. Still have no idea what happened to them. No one would talk to me — like if they did, they would be in danger. I couldn't control my temper, went after those guys, and then..."

He trailed off. There was no point in explaining any further; it was what it was.

"It's something that I'm going to have to live with," he said. "And sometimes it means nights like last night."

He turned and sat on the wall, waiting for

her response. Lena didn't say anything for a moment, only moved closer and put one soft hand on his chest. The way he'd done for her before.

Then she tilted her head critically, and said, "What do you mean, you 'got into it?'"

"What does that matter?"

"It matters. You said you lost your temper — what were they doing? Were they doing something horrible?"

Lena was doing it again. Looking at him like she could see through him. It was the weirdest thing he'd ever felt — to be *known* like that. By a sub.

"They were, weren't they?" she said.

"Well, yeah, they weren't nice guys, and I didn't lose my temper over nothing."

"Were they going after a woman?"

Now Chance was really flummoxed. He just looked at her, his mouth open slightly.

"Don't look at me like I'm a wizard or something," she said.

"*Are* you a wizard?" he laughed.

"I'm going to take that as a yes, they were doing something terrible to a woman," she said, her fingers tightening over his shirt. "Look, Chance, you have every right to grieve, and I can't even imagine how horrible that is. But don't beat yourself up for trying to *help* people."

~ * ~ * ~

Lena watched Chance's face closely. He clearly hadn't expected her to say all the things she'd said, but then, he didn't know that she'd gotten an assist from Lola. She wasn't sure what to expect in return. She had challenged his authority, in a way, but she was right. And he had to see it. In fact, she was sure he did see it, the look in his eyes—and then there was something else, something she couldn't decipher.

Something sad.

"There's something you're not telling me, isn't there?" she said.

Chance smiled at her, shaking his head a little. "Look at you," he said. "Yeah. There's something I'm not telling you."

"How is that fair?" she asked, starting to get kind of angry at him for his stupid stubbornness, even though she knew it wasn't her place—she had no claim on him. "You require honesty from me because otherwise what we're doing is dangerous, but you get a pass? How does that work?"

"It doesn't," he said.

Lena's heart fell to the floor. She shouldn't have said that. That was, in fact, a terrible thing to say, considering she was still keeping Paul Cigna's creepy texts from him. The last thing in the world she wanted was to hear that this arrangement, this thing that had given her new life, couldn't work.

"Don't say that," she said.

Chance stood up from the wall, and carefully, so carefully, took her in his arms. Lena could tell he was trying to be gentle, which made her feel sick. She didn't want him to *have* to be gentle about whatever he said next.

"But it's true, sweetheart," he said. "I told you, I don't have this totally figured out yet. This conversation was…premature. But this? This thing I'm not telling you? This is why I don't get involved, and I did get involved with you anyway because…oh shit, don't cry."

Lena was trying so, so hard not to, and she had no idea what was happening to her, just that this sounded like a breakup. It sounded like a breakup, and they weren't even together, and she didn't *want* the drama and the inevitable heartbreak that came with all that, either. She couldn't handle it. This arrangement had been perfect.

So why the hell was she crying?

"Hey," he said, brushing her tears away. "Don't cry, ok? I'm not finished. Just listen, all right?"

He looked so stricken, those blue eyes cloudy for the first time she could remember, that she actually felt bad. The last thing she wanted to do was cause him any pain, and she'd remembered too late that when she hurt, it affected him, too, because he was her Dom.

Oh God, please let him still be my Dom.

"Ignore me," she said, mimicking Lola's voice. She did her best to smile through the last of her tears.

Chance grinned. "You hormonal, too?"

"No, but I'm going to use it as an excuse."

His smile was like a light. "I won't tell."

But Lena found herself tugging at his shirt again, with the anxiety of not knowing rising within her. "Please, Chance, just…tell me what you need to say."

"Lena, I want to say I agreed to this because I wanted to help you, and that is true. I did. And I do. But it's more true to say… Jesus, Lena, I can't take my hands off of you. In a way that's new to me. I'm not like this with other subs. There is something that you do to me, beyond the sexual, beyond… But it doesn't matter. It's just not an ok way for this to happen."

"Why not?"

Chance frowned. "Look, I would never get into a scene with anyone if I felt I was unable to do so safely and responsibly. I can't tell you exactly how it works, but it puts me in a space…a different place. I'm in control there. I'm aware of my limitations as a man, and I don't mess with them when other people are involved. But there are things about me that aren't good. That are dangerous. And I don't know how that will affect things with you, because you're different. And there is nothing on this Earth that can make me put you at risk."

It was like someone had zapped her right in the head. Lena fisted his shirt in her hand, as if she could change his mind or lead him around or anything, really, because she did not like what she was hearing.

"It can't be anyone else but you," she said hoarsely. "It has to be you. I don't want anyone else. I don't trust anyone else."

Chance started to run his hands up and down her back again, in that soothing way that he had, and she shrugged it off.

"No, don't *soothe* me, just tell me you can still do this," she said, fighting back the tears again. She was clawing at his chest now, desperate and mindless. "You're the one I trust."

"Lena, the problem is, I don't know if you *should* trust me outside of a scene. I don't know if *I* should trust me. That's my fucking problem."

chapter 19

Chance had hated to leave Lena up there on the roof, but he had to do it. He had to go sort some things out on his own, for her sake. And, truly, for his own sake, too. So he'd sent Lola up to take care of her and then he'd gone straight to the gym.

Ten rounds on the heavy bag and he was only just *starting* to make sense of the whole thing.

Five minutes after leaving her, he'd felt like a dick for letting her believe he was some kind of noble, suffering hero. That was bullshit. The obvious solution was to just tell her about Jennie, about what Sean did to her, and about what he'd seen in himself since then — but then she kept going on about how she could only submit to him. Chance had been a Dom for a long time, and never with any problems, never with any cause for concern with anyone. It was when he was at his best. But everything felt different with Lena, and he wasn't sure how yet, wasn't sure what it meant, or if it would change things. So she calmed him — what would happen if something happened to her? Would it do the opposite? And telling her — would that take that away from her? Just so he could get it off his chest?

He pounded the bag in a non-stop flurry of combinations, knowing he'd just rationalized some stupid shit. The problem was that his feelings for Lena didn't stop when the scene did. And *that* was new to him, too.

By the time he'd worked himself into a full sweat he knew what he wanted to do. What his instincts were telling him to do.

They were telling him to tie Lena up and take his pleasure with her. That she was ready for it. That they needed to be closer, not further apart. He was always ok as a Dom. It would help him confirm what he thought — if he loved her.

Holy shit.

Chance stopped moving, the heavy bag swaying in front of him like a metronome, timing out the seconds since the word made itself heard in his head.

He rolled it around in his mind, trying to get the feel of it, the heft of it.

He loved Lena. And not just that. She made him...different. He knew that, fine. But he needed to know more.

And so did she. Maybe not the truth, just quite yet—he had to be perfectly sure before he started dropping bombs on her. She hadn't even been ready to open up to him yet about the things that had scarred her, she was skittish as hell, in her own words—"irrevocably skittish," she'd said—and he wouldn't risk hurting her more by shooting his mouth off just because it felt good and potentially sabotaging all her progress as a result.

But she damn well needed to see that he would be there. That he was her Dom.

Fuck. Going to the gym to work this off? Letting her suffer like this? It was stupid. It was fucking selfish. It was not who he was—he was a fucking Dom. He might be a lot of other things, too, many of them not good, but this was one thing he knew.

And he knew what Lena needed, at her core.

"Hey, Chance?"

"What?" he growled. He was already tearing off his gloves, ready to run back to Volare and do what needed to be done.

Billy was only slightly taken aback. "You in a hurry?"

"Yes."

"Ok. Yeah, well, I don't think Mikey's gonna train with you no more. It's nothing personal,

Chance, but the boy's been asking so many questions. It's not just the gloves this time, it's all this…this sex stuff. I don't know. I'm gonna send him to computer camp and just…"

Chance looked at the old man. He couldn't blame him, even though Chance felt that he was wrong. Chance knew some people would always see him differently because of Volare, and some people would always see him differently because of his violent past.

"That's fine," Chance said.

"No hard feelings?"

"None."

"Well, all right then. Chance?"

Chance turned, already seething, wanting to be on his way. "Yeah?"

"She seems like a lovely girl."

"She is."

Chance made it back to Volare in under a minute, jogging the last few yards, practically running into Lola on his way through.

"Hey!" she said, sidestepping in front of him, blocking his way. "I want to talk to you!"

"Now?"

"Yes, now. You're being an idiot. Being a responsible Dom isn't about *not* getting involved, it's about being in control and aware of your involvement. And I know you've got special concern because of Jennie Sands, but honestly, Chance, you're not like that. It doesn't mean you can't care about a sub, or fall in love, or whatever. Where would Roman and I be if we were that dumb? Or, you know, had stayed that dumb? Don't run away—"

"Oh, *Christ*, Lola, I *know*. Now I love you, but get the hell out of my way," Chance said. "You're standing between me and my sub."

~ * ~ * ~

There were a whole lot of things in the world that Lena did not understand. First, there was Chance. Apparently. She loved him as Dom. Loved how even when he was letting her get away with being a smartass, or letting her tease him, or whatever, there was always this rumbling undercurrent of...Dom. She teased him at his pleasure. Part of the fun was knowing that there would eventually be consequences.

And yet so much of what he did was for *her*. He owned her, and he...he cherished her.

He'd used the word. She just hadn't made the connection.

And now he wasn't? Anymore? For some reason she didn't understand. And she'd had the gall to yell at him—to *yell* at him—for keeping something from her when she'd been keeping Paul Cigna's harassment from him the whole time.

She'd gotten another text. The timing, as always, was impeccable. It was like Cigna knew when she was already down and just couldn't resist. But this one had been, by far, the worst: "Play it your way. But I have more pictures."

More pictures.

Lena had already been going kind of nuts, freaking out about Chance, wanting him back under any circumstances and not willing to reflect too deeply on why, but now? Now she was freaking out about Chance *and* the idea that there were more pictures. She couldn't get it out of her head.

She couldn't stop thinking about what they contained. How much worse they might be.

If she knew Richie, he'd be savvy about the whole thing. He was shallow and selfish, not stupid. It made sense now — he'd release the first batch, then wait until coverage was ebbing, then release the really shocking ones, just to prolong his little media party, thinking maybe he could get a new career out of it. He already *had* a new career out of it — that part in Roddy Nichols' new film.

If Lena hadn't already been convinced that karma was a complete farce, she would be now. She had worked herself into a complete mess by the time Chance came through her door.

They stared at each other for a moment. No, she stared at him, hopeful. He *studied* her. That stare. That Dom stare, where his eyes seemed alive and predatory. Evaluating, learning, making decisions about what would happen to her.

"You're upset," he said.

The *voice*.

"Yes," she said.

"Because of the things I said," he said. "And didn't say?"

"Because of a lot of things," she said. The look on his face made her so, so hopeful. She couldn't imagine anything better than having him back right now. She wanted it more than anything.

"I made a mistake," he said, his eyes holding her locked in place. "With you. I don't often do that. But I'm here to rectify that now."

A shiver started in her sex and rippled through Lena's entire body as he walked around her.

"Thank you," she said.

She was so grateful just to see him. So grateful to notice the black bag he'd brought into her bedroom, the bag that carried so many of his tools, and to know what it meant.

A wave of anxiety returned. She had to double check.

"Chance, does this mean you're back? That we're still…"

Lena faltered on the words. She wasn't used to that. She could always find the words to articulate what she felt, to describe a scene, to get her point across. Maybe it wasn't finding the words that was the problem—maybe it was the words themselves. She wasn't supposed to be attached, she wasn't supposed to make this into more than it was, she wasn't supposed to depend on him for more than this one thing.

"Lena," he said, walking toward her, his eyes never leaving hers. "I am your Dom. You are my sub. And I am not going anywhere."

His voice was like iron. Something solid, something real that she could hold on to, and her sense of relief was...oh God, she was going to cry. She willed herself calm. She wanted him, right now, more than anything. She wanted him to show her that he was her Dom. She wanted to feel that combination of pleasure and pain, of helplessness and safety, of knowing she was under his complete control—that at least in this one area, she was safe, because she was his.

She couldn't do anything about those new pictures; she couldn't do anything about what would happen. But she could submit to Chance.

He stepped closer to her, and she saw he was covered in sweat, gleaming. It made her think of sex. It made her think of that first night, in the roof garden, the way he'd been just a hungry animal, the way he'd helped her to give in to what she wanted.

"I've been preparing you, Lena," he said.

"Helping you to feel comfortable. Helping you learn. But now I'm going to take you for me. Because I want you. Because you are mine. And because you need to know that."

Mine.

That sent shockwaves right through her. She did need to know that. She needed to know he was still her Dom, that this—this thing that felt like the only thing she had left—that this wasn't being taken from her, too. Relief. So much relief. Enough relief to cover the twinge of anxiety that she felt when she thought about what any of that meant, really meant, for her. She just wanted the relief. She just wanted to forget about the mess her life had become.

She just wanted him.

"Why are you almost crying?" he asked.

"I'm relieved," she said. "I'm so relieved. I can't do this with anyone else. At least not yet."

Why had she said that? She'd never even thought about—

Chance's nostrils flared, his eyes flashed, and he stepped closer. Studying her again. Assessing.

"I'm sorry I gave you reason to question me, or to think I'd abandon you," he finally said. "That was wrong. But you are *my* sub, no one else's, and I'm going to show it to you."

A current raced through her, an actual live current, and every single nerve in her body cried out for more. Yes. This. Him.

Now.

Chance held her by the back of the neck and claimed her mouth, his tongue roving, licking, probing—taking. Lena's body drew to his all on its own, her lips tender and alive, her mouth dissolving into his. He pulled back, his large hand holding her in place, and gave her a ferocious look.

"Mine," he said.

He freed her briefly to grab the bottom of her t-shirt; she didn't need to be told to lift her arms. He stripped it off of her and tore off her bra, throwing them aside, and placed his hand back on her neck. He lifted one breast, taking the nipple in his mouth, sucking and biting just enough to make it sting, then did the same to the other. He left them tingling and aching, demanding to be touched, and looked her again in the eye.

"Mine," he said.

He hooked his thumbs in the waistband of her comfy old sweatpants, found her underwear there—frowned—and then stripped her of both. She stepped out of the pile of clothing without a word, and when he put his foot between hers, she spread her legs.

He thrust his hand between her legs, one finger dallying in her wetness, and then he gripped her there.

"Mine," he rasped.

She felt her legs go weak.

Without warning, Chance spun her around, his arm like an iron bar across her chest holding her immobile, and bent her slightly forward. He smoothed one hand across her butt, then spread her cheeks and pressed a finger against her anus.

"Mine," he growled.

Lena's body was jerking in slight, small random contractions, like parts of her were all ready to come right away, and all she could think of was how long it would be until he was inside her. Until he *took* all of those things.

She felt his lips at her ear, his warm breath on her neck.

"And I want what is mine," he said.

chapter 21

Chance led her through his bedroom and on to his private playroom, his hand grasped around her wrists, not wanting to let go of her at all. Lena was soaring. She couldn't think of anything better, of anything that could possibly have made her feel better than she did right now. Moments ago she'd thought Chance was gone, and she was freaking out about new pictures.

Now she had Chance. Or Chance had her.

He wants what's his.

Those words…

She wanted to be taken. More than anything. And when she saw what was set up in this room, she sank into the slight fear and let it strengthen her arousal. Subspace was so freeing. So close.

There was a wedge-shaped mat in the center of the room with a raised pillow on the high end, like one of those cylindrical pillows she remembered from yoga classes. There were little ledges on the sides, she guessed for her knees, and rings bolted in everywhere for...

Restraints.

She took a few deep breaths and knew she was wet.

Chance walked over to the high end of the wedge and looked at her. "Come here," he commanded.

She did. She saw she was trembling as she did so, her mind feeling scattered, jumpy, not the empty calm she was so used to. Chance put a hand to her face, felt her neck, her chest, stroked her back.

"Lena, I'm checking in," he said.

"Green," she said without hesitation. She would get there. She needed to.

He stared at her for a moment longer, his eyes narrowing. Finally, he said, "Put your knees here and bend over the pillow."

Even as eager as she was, there was something frightening about climbing up on a piece of equipment like this. It was like training hard to take a lone skydive in a remote place—when the moment came, the door open and the abyss below, even the most excited thrill junky would feel that fear. Lena was still eager to take the plunge. She saw immediately, as she positioned herself, that her legs were spread wide and bent as far as they would go, her heels jutting into her thighs, up near the level her chest would be at when she leaned over, her butt high in the air — leaving her more spread, more open, more vulnerable than she'd ever been before. He cuffed her ankles, and she knew she wasn't moving.

She could barely contain herself.

She leaned into it, spreading her arms out in front of her, pressing her chest into the padded wedge and pushing her butt up in the air as high as it would go.

God she wanted him.

Smack.

He'd spanked her once — just once. She started.

"Don't take liberties," he said, caressing her ass. "This is mine."

Lena gasped, smiling, turning her face to the side and resting it on the padded surface.

"Put your hands behind your back," he said.

Lena did so, slowly. She wasn't hesitant, but she wasn't prepared for how much it would shake her balance — with her hands behind her back, she was completely, *completely* powerless. She had zero leverage. She couldn't move, couldn't struggle, couldn't adjust, couldn't do anything at all unless he did it to her.

When she felt the soft leather cuffs go around her wrists, she could have sworn it was like he'd touched her clit. She moaned softly, silently begging him to touch her, and it got even worse when she heard him chuckle. She was so swollen that she hurt. Her pulse throbbed around her clit and she wasn't allowed to move.

Torture.

"I can see that you like this, huh?" he said. "That's good, because so do I. We'll spend lots of time like this."

"Please," she gasped. "Chance, I feel like I'm going to burst."

"Soon," he said, and she felt the first drops of lube fall on her tight, exposed ass.

She held her breath until she felt it. First his finger, insistent and firm, stretching her. Then the plastic, only bigger this time. Much bigger.

Oh God.

"Breathe out, bear down," he ordered.

Lena closed her eyes, exhaled, and pushed. It stretched against her until she thought it was too much, until it hurt and she was certain he'd made a mistake, there was just no way at all, it was impossible...

"Oh!" she cried as he pushed it past the tight ring of muscle, filling her more than she thought she could stand. It wasn't immediately comfortable, but she could feel herself starting to relax around it, to mold herself to this thing he'd put inside her.

It was overwhelming.

"You're almost there," he said, from behind her. "Soon, and I'll have this, too. But for now…"

Oh God, what was he going to do? Her nipples ached, her pussy ached, her body felt full and yet empty at the same time, and all she wanted was him. She knew that as soon as he entered her she'd hit that space, she'd hit that calm, and she'd be…

She'd be all right.

She didn't expect the blindfold. It wasn't such a big thing, not in the scheme of things, not considering how she was bound and spread and already at his mercy. But when Chance blindfolded her there was a sudden stab, a pang of panic, intruding on her, on their scene, taking her right out of it. Intruding on this thing she wanted so badly, this thing she needed—thoughts of the new photos.

She'd been blindfolded and bound with Richie, too, and now all she could think about was what pictures he'd taken then. What else hadn't she known about? Was she about to find out?

And she couldn't stop it. She couldn't stop her mind from going to this hated place, she couldn't stop it from taking this scene away from her, and she wanted Chance *so badly*…

"Lena." Chance's voice was the only thing to break through. She reached for it desperately.

He said, "Red."

What?

The blindfold came off. The cuffs came off. Slowly, so slowly, the butt plug came out. She didn't move except to turn her head to look for Chance, only to find him by her side, lifting her gingerly from the wedge. He picked her up the way he had so many times before and carried her back towards his bedroom.

"Chance," she said, struggling to find her voice. "What's happening?"

"I used a safeword, sweetheart. I ended the scene, because you were not ok."

He settled them both in his favorite chair, holding her huddled against his chest, and it was then that Lena realized her heart was racing. Her limbs were cold. She was sweating a little.

He was right.

She was not ok.

~ * ~ * ~

Lena huddled against his chest, confused and bewildered. She hadn't started to show symptoms of a panic attack until she'd been safe in his arms—something he had seen before. Some people functioned extremely well when exposed to a stressor and only felt the detrimental effects of that stress later, when they were safe. She was one of them. He wondered bitterly where she'd had to develop that particular skill.

He'd first sensed that something was wrong when he'd brought her up to the wedge and looked in her eyes. There wasn't anything concrete, and it he wouldn't have been able to explain it if anyone asked, but he had known something wasn't right. So he'd chucked his original plans out the window and focused on her.

When he checked in and she gave that eager but unfocused "green," he realized he'd have to go through the preparations for a scene, as gently as possible, until she herself realized what was wrong. Or at least acknowledged that there was *something* was wrong — otherwise she would have experienced his stopping the scene as just another rejection.

So he'd watched her. And it was the blindfold that put her over the edge.

Chance tried to focus on the positive — he knew this would be a moment for her, that something was rising to the surface. She'd have something to tell him, and that meant progress. Probably.

But he hated to see her upset. Loathed it. He couldn't rub her back or kiss her forehead or hold her tight enough.

"You ok to talk?" he asked her.

"I think so," she said, lifting her head off of her chest. "How did you know? I mean, I didn't...I wouldn't have said it, but you were right."

"You weren't you. Set my Dom sense off."

She smiled. "Dom sense?"

"With great power comes great responsibility," he said sagely. He loved how Lena could circle in to something important, never forgetting her sense of humor. But now she was going to have to deal with the hard stuff.

"What happened when I put the blindfold on you?" he asked.

Chance expected to see stress in her eyes. But not fear. Fear directed at him. Whatever it was, she was afraid to tell him.

"I'm so sorry," she said.

"You have nothing to apologize for."

"Except that I do," she said. "I am a total fucking hypocrite. I yelled at you for keeping things from me, and the whole time I was thinking, 'You jerk, you're keeping things from him, too.'"

Big breath.

"I've been getting these texts," she said.

A million things clicked into place at once. The way she would become stressed out of nowhere, the continued response to Paul Cigna as opposed to Richie Kerns...

"Paul Cigna," Chance said. He was very, very careful to keep his voice calm.

"I assume. I don't know. Unknown

number."

Chance tilted up her face toward his again, determined not to let her hide from him—and she was hiding, like she couldn't bear to see his reaction. Like she was afraid he would be mad at her. Chance was angry—Jesus, was he angry—but not at her.

"Lena, stop being afraid," he said, and let his thumb brush gently against her lower lip. "I'm not angry with you. I'm not disappointed. I'm worried. Why didn't you tell me?"

"I…"

He'd stumped her. Those big hazel eyes were more open and raw than he'd ever seen them.

"I didn't want it to be real," she said finally. "And I didn't want to impose…"

"You can't impose on me, Lena," he said. "No matter how hard you might try. I promise you that."

Chance was more distressed about that than he let on—his early attempts to be honest and upfront about what he believed to be his obligation not to get emotionally involved with Lena had contributed to this. He hadn't known she had such issues about trusting people to stick around when he'd said all that crap, otherwise he would have framed it differently. As it was, though, it wasn't like he could turn back time. He'd have to work to convince her he wasn't going anywhere, but in the meantime, there was Paul Cigna to deal with. One problem at a time.

"What did they say?" he asked her. She seemed relieved to move on to practical stuff, wiping at her eyes and getting some color back in her face.

"I don't know, like, taunting, I guess? Trying to get me to come out or comment on you. But the last one I got this afternoon—"

While he was at the gym. Of fucking course.

"—said there were more pictures. And I just kept thinking about what could be in them. If he took them when I was blindfolded."

He felt her stiffen first, as though just speaking the words aloud did, in fact, make it more real. Chance forced himself to calm down, to keep his own body relaxed, just because he didn't want to add to her stress.

But holy shit, he was pissed.

This was the first time he'd felt that old urge to go destroy something evil while in the company of Lena. The first time he'd gotten the itch, the burning along his limbs, the tightness in his gut.

"Chance?" she said, her voice tiny. "Please don't—"

"I'm not going to do anything stupid, Lena," he said. "But that doesn't mean I'm going to allow this to continue, either."

chapter 21

Chance had finally gotten her to sleep. He'd had to wait, buzzing inside like an entire hive of pissed off killer bees, while she finally let her own exhaustion overtake her and drifted off. And she *was* exhausted—hiding stuff like that put a strain on her, like it would anyone. Chance knew that from experience.

But it wasn't really the time to be laying more stuff at her feet. What he could do, though, was solve this particular problem for her. Emotional scars didn't respond to threats from big, military-trained men. Cowards with cameras did.

Chance pounded on Ford's office door, thankful they'd had the foresight to give the lawyer an on-site office. He didn't expect to find it full.

"What the hell?" he said. Ford, Adra, and Declan Donovan were all looking at him like he'd caught them at something. He did not have time for this.

"We were just putting together a plan for you to approve," Ford said, getting to his feet. "We weren't going to bother you until we had everything in place."

"Ford, I need an opinion on something. In private. Now."

The room chilled under the influence of far too much testosterone. Pissing matches between Doms were rare at Volare, mostly because Chance thought they were stupid and didn't tolerate them, but it was instinctual to bristle at a challenge. They must have seen something in Chance's face, because both Ford and Declan brought themselves down.

"No worries," Declan said, standing up. "Ford and Adra have agreed to help me rehabilitate my image, and I want the club to be part of it. Needs your approval eventually— I'm not going to bring the club into it without that. We'll talk later."

Chance watched silently as Declan escorted a meek-looking Adra out, knowing he was being a complete dick. He didn't really care at this point. More important things to do.

"Ford," he said.

Ford's gaze was still focused on Adra—or on Declan's hand on the small of Adra's back.

The man did not look happy.

"Ford, get your goddamn head in the game," Chance said.

"What do you want, Chance?"

"I need to know what happens to the club if I get in trouble."

That got Ford's attention. He ran his hand through his blond hair and sat back down, saying, "Well, shit. What are you talking about?"

"There's something I need to take care of," Chance said.

"I'm your lawyer, Chance. Don't beat around the bush, it's a waste of time."

"Paparazzi scum are harassing Lena. I'm going to stop them."

"Meaning?"

Chance wanted to be able to say he was just going to scare them, or bribe them, or bribe them and scare them—whatever worked. That's what his intent was, anyway. He gritted his teeth.

"Meaning I'm going to find them and get them to stop. Dudes with cameras sometimes make a fuss about stuff like that, but I'm not putting up with this. What's the club's liability if they come out swinging or make accusations?"

Ford shrugged. "If worse came to worst, you might have to resign for insurance purposes. But the club doesn't have any direct liability. We're not going to get sued if you go off and do something stupid on your own time."

"Excellent," Chance said.

A couple of phone calls, and Chance had the information he needed. Paul Cigna of the peeping camera and dipshit hat had been seen tailing Richie Kerns almost exclusively. And Richie had been spending his nights hanging out at Kendo, some new club where people tried hard to be seen.

Ergo, Chance was going to Kendo.

He was also trying very, very hard to maintain that sense of calm. That Lena Zen. Because these were two douchebags who really deserved to face some painful consequences.

And there one of them was: dumb blue hat, camera around his neck, cigarette in his mouth, hanging out on the corner like he wasn't a piece of crap. Chance parked a block or two down and made for Paul Cigna in a direct line. He didn't care if Paul made him, or if Paul ran. He'd catch him.

Or, as luck would have it, he'd just grab him by the arm and drag him into the trashed alley next to the club.

"Hey what the hell?" Paul sputtered. "Look, don't take the camera, ok? I'll go to the ATM and get..."

And then he saw Chance's face.

"Oh shit."

"Yeah, oh shit," Chance said. "Call him. Right now. Get him out here."

"Who?"

Paul actually looked like he thought that would work.

"Don't mess with me, Paul, it's going to make me angry. Your buddy, Richie. Call him, get him out here, right fucking now."

Chance didn't touch him. He just…loomed. And thought very hard about punching Paul in the gut.

The message must have gotten through.

"Yeah, ok, Jesus Christ. But he's probably coked up. I can't do anything about that."

They didn't have to wait. Richie definitely had something going with Paul—otherwise they wouldn't have been attached at the hip, and Richie wouldn't have come spilling out the side door into an alley that smelled like piss and rot, all eager to talk to Paul.

Well, eager until he saw Chance, anyway.

"Paul, what the—"

Chance shoved him into the dirty wall and held him there. Not hard. Just enough to let him know he could pick him up and launch him over the goddamn building if he felt like it.

"I don't want either of you to speak until spoken to. This is for your own safety. There is nothing I want more than to end both of you right now, so please, for all of our sakes, do not fucking test me. Say you understand."

Richie looked like he was about to piss himself. Paul Cigna only looked impatient, like he wanted to get something over with.

"We get it," Paul said. "What do you want?"

"I want to know why you've been stalking Lena Simone Maddox."

"Ok, first thing," Paul said, lighting up another cigarette. "I am not a *stalker*, for Chrissakes. I don't sit around writing letters and collecting hairbrushes like some lonely freak. I'm a professional."

Chance's anger was rising. This man didn't take what he'd done seriously. Just casually dismissed all the damage he'd done to another human being, like his lack of infatuation somehow made it better. Like any of that mattered to the person he'd hunted.

Chance grabbed the cigarette out of Paul's mouth. It hissed against his hand as it went out, and Paul's mouth dropped open.

"Not in the mood," Chance said. "I don't care what you call yourself. But if you don't tell me what's going on right now, I swear to God —"

"Jesus, dude," Paul squeaked. "Richie doesn't pay me enough for this. It's his thing, not mine. He paid me to keep it up."

Chance reeled, and looked back at Richie to find the man actually blubbering. "What?

Why?"

With shaking hands, Paul Cigna lit his third cigarette. "He wants the publicity. Wants a new career. Wanted your girl to flip out, do something nuts, keep the story going any way he could." He shrugged, cigarette glowing. "It's just a job."

Chance saw red.

Later, he remembered the smell of the cigarette.

He remembered the feel of Paul Cigna's bony wrist in his hand as he twisted him around and slammed him into the wall.

He remembered the blue fedora falling into a puddle of foul liquid leaking off in a trail from a pile of garbage bags.

There was Richie Kerns, shouting, and Paul Cigna, begging. There was the sound of his own blood rushing in his ears, his breathing echoing in his head, and the knowledge that this man had psychologically tortured Lena with the hope that she'd crack and it would make for good entertainment.

And then there was Lena. Ever-present in his mind.

The Zen of Lena.

What would happen to Lena if he broke this man's arm, face, whatever?

He let Paul Cigna go.

"You fucking *psycho*—" the pap said as he stumbled away from Chance, trying to find a

CHLOE COX

scrap of dignity somewhere on the alley floor.

"Don't," Chance said, rolling his head from side to side. "Just give me the remaining pictures, and we'll be done."

"How about you go fuck yourself?"

"Interesting counteroffer," Chance said. He was losing his patience. "Let's see what I can come up with."

"Hey guys!"

It was Richie Kerns, the idiot with sunglasses hanging from his shirt, holding his hands spread wide like he had a big idea. All of a sudden, the jackass felt empowered. He'd been quietly whimpering against the wall the whole time, and now he had an idea? Chance hadn't even let himself contemplate Richie Kerns. Or rather, Richie Kerns and Lena. He didn't trust himself to do that, so being forced to talk to him like a human person wasn't Chance's favorite thing to do.

"What?" Chance growled.

"Look, dude? I get it, ok. She's your girl now, I see how that's awkward. But you're not looking at this from the right perspective. You gotta help her see the light, man."

"Richie, shut up," muttered Paul.

Chance wondered at what was happening now. It was almost as if Richie's drug addled brain had just kicked into gear, but wasn't quite caught up.

"No, it's cool, I got this. He just doesn't get

it." Richie smiled at Chance. He probably thought it was charming. "You have to talk to her, man. She's being so dumb. I mean, come on, right, we all know she's never going to be a serious actress or whatever, and nobody gives a shit about what she writes. That's just how it is. She's hot, and that's what people want to see, and those pictures made her actually almost famous. She could be making a freaking fortune if she'd only work with me on this!"

"He happens to be right, you know," Paul said, looking for his matches somewhere on the ground. He'd dropped them when Chance had briefly flirted with the idea of kicking his ass. "He's an idiot, but he's right about this. She's never going to be anything other than what she is. She might as well capitalize on it. But if you're going to beat someone up for making the suggestion, I would encourage you to go after Richie."

Richie cursed. "Paul, c'mon, man. Why?"

Chance ran his hand over his head, his mind spinning as things clicked into place. This attitude: this was what Lena thought, too. No faith in her. No one had faith in her, not even Lena. Especially not Lena, not anymore.

Because of people like this.

"How much for the photos?" Chance said. "All of them. Every copy."

"No, dude, you don't get it—"

"Richie, shut up," Paul said. He was smiling

in the evil glow from his cigarette. "Mr. Dalton, Richie doesn't have any pictures. He gave them all to me as part of our deal. You're willing to pay to for them?"

"Yes."

"Paul, what the hell? What about me?" Richie complained.

"No one cares, Richie. This has been a bust. And I want to make a profit on this somehow," Paul said, dropping his cigarette and squishing it like a bug. Chance hated how smug the man was. "I'll be in touch, Mr. Dalton."

chapter 22

Lena completed her millionth lap of Chance's roof garden, taking another peek over the side to see if his car was approaching.

Nope. Still not there.

He'd left her another note, but it was, as notes went, pretty terrible. "Be back soon?" Crappy note. Lola had laughed and said that was about as good as he got in the note department.

Lena had used the time to prepare. Or to try to. She was getting more and more irritated that Richie and Paul Cigna had managed to take that bondage scene away from her. As messed up as she'd been, that position…God. She'd been so helpless, so open. Knowing that Chance could do anything he wanted to her in that position, anything at all…

And she hadn't gotten to enjoy it. And neither had Chance.

It was maybe a minor thing to focus on, given all the crap that had happened already, but for some reason it was the final straw. Lena's frustration was only compounded by the fact that she was worried. Not just worried about Chance—though, honestly, given his tendency to run around taking on people who hurt her, she was pretty worried—but worried and regretful, over her own behavior.

Lena knew she had been stupid. And neurotic. And all kinds of messed up. It was a fantasy to pretend that she wasn't already dependent on Chance in some very important ways, that she wasn't emotionally involved, that he didn't own a very important part of her. But knowing that it was stupid, that it didn't make sense, and that it wasn't helpful did absolutely nothing to stop the feelings of dread and panic that she continually had to fight off when she tried to acknowledge that fact.

The truth was, in Lena's world, when you depended on someone—when you loved them—that was when everything would fall apart. The only person in her life who hadn't done that yet was Thea. Lena didn't know if she'd ever be able to shake that fear, but she did know that she wanted to, for Chance. Chance deserved better.

She had no idea if he really wanted her, or would ever really want her, or what the hell was going on, but she did know that Chance deserved much better, even if he was convinced he couldn't be with anyone.

Talk about screwed up.

"What a pair," she said to herself.

"Which pair are we talking about?" Chance said from behind her. "If it's the one I'm thinking of," he said, letting his eyes roam, "I would have to agree."

Lena just stared at him and his grin. Then she laughed, in spite of how annoyed she was. He could always get her to laugh.

"Where the hell were you?" she demanded. But before he could tell her, she'd launched herself up into his arms, wrapping herself around him in a big kiss.

"Hey, I left a note," he said.

"Leave better notes. No, seriously, I'm mad at you," she said. She really was annoyed, and yet just could not keep her hands off of him.

"I went to go take care of the picture situation," Chance said, setting her down. His face had changed. Darkened. "I'm not ok with those bastards dogging you indefinitely. That is not your life, and you are not under their control. You should be able to make whatever choices you want without being afraid."

Lena didn't quite know what to say. On the one hand, something deep inside of her swooned at the idea of Chance standing up for her like that—again. That he'd make it his mission to protect her, to, like, *avenge* her? Yes, swoon. Many, many swoons. But truly, at the same time? It wasn't the middle ages, and nothing Chance could do to Paul Cigna or Richie Kerns would help Lena to feel any differently about the things that had already happened.

"Chance," she said, putting her hand to his face. She loved his skin. "Thank you, but—"

"Wait," he said, taking hold of her hand. "There's something I need to tell you. You need to listen first."

That last sentence—the Dom voice. Would she ever not respond to it? He was like a hypnotist, it was insane. But his eyes weren't the usual clear, bright, piercing blue. Instead they were mercurial, like they had been when he'd told her their arrangement couldn't work, and instantly Lena froze.

She struggled to fight down the panic.

"Ok," she said. Her voice sounded brittle. Chance frowned.

"Sweetheart, it's not that," he said gently. "Look at me. Stop worrying. I told you I wasn't going anywhere."

And with that, he kissed her. Soft, warm, sweet. His hand on her cheek, his body close to hers.

Calming.

"You were going to say that taking care of Paul and Richie doesn't fix everything, weren't you?" he asked.

How did he do that? Honestly?

"Yes," she said.

"Yeah, well, believe me, I know all about that," Chance said, sitting down on one of the couches and pulling Lena onto his lap. "All right, so the thing I wasn't telling you is this. My first serious girlfriend was a girl named Jennie Sands, and I was a dick to her. Broke her heart, treated her badly. Not on purpose, but man, was I dumb. And then I got offended when people tried to point out that I was being an asshole."

"So you were being a teenager?"

"Don't make excuses for me. Nineteen is old enough to know better. Anyway, I broke Jennie's heart and made her feel like crap, and so she started dating this loser named Sean Morrigan. I didn't care one way or another, ignored her when she tried to get my attention, continued my general cocky asshole behavior, totally self-absorbed and not thinking about anyone but myself. I enlisted, and when I came back, Jennie was dead."

Lena had been about to speak, but now she just sat there, staring at Chance with her mouth open. He smiled sadly and held her with those eyes.

"Yeah. Sean Morrigan beat her. Badly. Had

been, the whole time I'd been ignoring her. One day he hit her hard enough that she fell back and smacked her head on the corner of a table. Don't say it's not my fault," Chance said, preempting her. "I know there's no direct line between me treating her like crap and Sean Morrigan being an abusive piece of crap. And I'm not saying that if it hadn't been for me she wouldn't have gotten into that situation, and I'm not saying…shit. I just don't know, do I? It certainly wasn't her fault. How close is anyone, at their most vulnerable point, to getting into bad situations they wouldn't get into otherwise?"

Lena traced the line of his jaw with her fingertip, unable to look away. Chance wanted her to see everything.

"That's actually something I know all about myself," she said quietly.

"After that, I went off the rails for a while. Like I did in Nigeria. I've been in a lot of fights, a lot of physical altercations, every time I see anything that even comes close… It's like I've been trying to make up for not being around when Jennie needed someone. It's not normal, the feeling I get in those situations," he said.

"No, I wouldn't think so," Lena said. "They aren't normal situations."

"You asked me what my number one fear was, remember?"

"Yeah. I only got fear number three."

Chance smiled, and tucked Lena's hair behind her ear. "Yeah, well, fear number one is that I'm like those guys, only with a different finish. Just the other side of the same coin."

Lena thought back to when she'd tried to take control by confronting Paul Cigna, how she'd wondered if, for her, giving up sexual control to Chance was a way of gaining control over her life. She thought she understood about coins and sides. She frowned.

"That's not you," she said.

"Don't argue," he said, and those sea glass blue eyes flashed. "That's not something I'd ever ask anyone else to be a part of. Hence not being able to get involved. Except I fucked up, Lena, because I love you anyway."

Everything.

Just.

Stopped.

Lena felt too many things at once, too many to count or identify, like a flock of fluttering, nervous birds crowding her inside her head, and so she sat there, quiet and still, and tried not to frighten them away.

It didn't work.

The flock exploded outwards and inwards all at once, whirling her around, tossing her between elation—oh God, so much elation—and disbelief, and confusion—so much confusion—and, as always, sullen and immovable, the dread she carried within her that anyone who loved her would inevitably turn against her.

"Lena," Chance said, very intently. "Look at me."

As if she could look anywhere else.

"You don't have to say anything to that right now. In fact, you're not allowed to yet. You have to think on it without all this stuff going on. But I'm still going to take care of you. I'm going to protect you. And I'm going to help you as much as I can."

Lena licked her lips and swallowed, trying to wet her suddenly dry throat, trying not to choke on the immense gratitude she felt for how he'd just let her off the hook. If he'd stormed up there declaring he loved her and demanding something from her in return, she knew that she would have bolted in a complete panic, leaving a Lena-sized hole in the door on her way to find someplace to hide.

As it was she was pulled tight between dread and devotion, and all that was left, loud enough to make itself heard, was how much she wanted him. How much she wanted him to dominate her. How much she wanted that scene she'd been robbed of. That peace.

"I don't want to think about anyone else when I see a blindfold," she whispered.

"I know, sweetheart," Chance said. "That's why I'm going to give you something else to think about. I'm going to take what's mine."

Lena stood in Chance's bedroom, naked and alone. He'd led her there, ordered her to strip and to wait, and then he'd gone…somewhere. To get things. Toys. Equipment.

Waiting was torture. Waiting let her mind wander. Waiting let her think, over and over again, about what he was going to do.

And she knew it was on purpose. She knew that Chance knew exactly what he was doing. Diabolical, brilliant, beautiful man.

But he didn't know about the war going on inside of her, between her rational, cynical side and her heart. Her inner cynic was screaming at her to run. Just get the hell out of there before the inevitable happened.

Her heart…

Lena didn't know. She wanted to be good enough for him. She wanted to be good enough to love him in the way he deserved.

She was just to the point of worrying that these preoccupations, that this anxiety about it all, would intrude on her thoughts and poison the scene all over again when she heard the door open behind her.

"Close your eyes," he said.

And this time, knowing that Chance was doing something about the pictures, that voice banished all of those thoughts. Just gone. Lena could grab a hold of that voice and ride the moment.

God, she was grateful. Screw the rest. She'd figure it out later.

She could hear him moving around the room, messing with equipment, making things ready. Something clinked. Metal on metal. Not being able to see, not *knowing*, was so much worse than simply waiting. It left her mind empty, and so she had to fill it with all sorts of thoughts...

"Put your hands behind your back."

Lena did, and the feel of the now familiar leather cuffs made her shudder. She wondered if her nipples were peaked. They ached, so they must have been.

And then she felt the blindfold come down. She'd obediently kept her eyes closed, but that was different—she knew she could open them at any time.

Now she was one step closer towards utter helplessness.

So it was that the first sensation on her skin made her gasp, even though it was feather light, just a small, delicate, soft caress, trailing down the front of her body. It tickled. It made her breathing speed up, it put every nerve in her body on high alert.

Then came the sharp sting on her nipple.

Lena squealed.

A flogger? A crop?

Her muscles tensed. She could have sworn her hearing had improved, and her sense of smell—she could smell Chance, that male musk that was only his. But he didn't speak, he didn't explain, he didn't warn. She had no idea what the next sensation would be, or where, or how it would feel.

She was pretty sure she was shaking.

"Oh *God*," she cried, half-laughing as the feather came between her legs from behind, darted in and out, gone before she could totally process what had happened.

Then several sharp blows to her ass, one, two, three, each one spiking pain and pleasure to her clit. She could feel her pulse between her legs again, could feel it start to build and swell.

She so badly wanted to see him, wanted to be able to prepare for whatever came next. In the past she'd hadn't been able to relax enough into being blindfolded to truly appreciate how powerless she felt without sight. It was the one sense she depended upon the most, the one thing she absolutely needed to make sense of the world, and she'd given it to him.

She was utterly, completely, under his power.

chapter 23

"Walk forward," he said.

His hand was flat on her back, pushing her and guiding her at the same time. Walking was another thing she didn't expect to be so difficult, but just the act of putting one foot in front of the other took on new significance without sight—and without arms. Hers were still very effectively bound behind her.

It felt like an eternity before her legs bumped up against Chance's bed. Everything felt different, alien.

Even frightening. Frightening, and yet safe, with Chance.

"One knee up," he said, his other hand on her stomach now, balancing her. "Then the other."

Climbing up on a bed was surprisingly

difficult with bound hands. And blindfolded. Everything, *everything*, seemed calculated to emphasize how helpless she was.

How needy she was.

How much she wanted him, inside her.

His hands applied pressure, bending her at the waist until her chest and shoulders came into contact with something soft — pillows? She turned her to the side and tried to relax. It left her ass up in the air, her knees apart, her arms behind her back, and her cheek pressed into cool, soft linen.

Open. Vulnerable.

She didn't think she'd be able to get up on her own — she'd lose her balance and fall, blindly. That feeling of not being able to move was more restraining than any chains or cuffs. She wouldn't move until he was done with her.

Oh God.

Drops of thick, cold lube fell on her ass, and she clenched at the thought of what would happen next, what he promised her would happen — if he wanted her ass, it was his for the taking, served up right in front of him.

He chuckled. "Not yet."

Instead there was the now familiar feel of a plug, even bigger than the last time. She whimpered, and he slipped a finger inside her vagina, as though just to say hi. He laughed when she bore down on him, a reflex at this point.

CHLOE COX

"You can do this," he said. "Relax into it."

She thought of all the other times he'd done this, how each time there was a moment when she was sure it was impossible, and did her best to relax. This one was worse, for that moment, bigger and tougher, and her body resisted—until it didn't.

She gave a small little cry as the plug filled her, jolting awake a part of her body that was still new to this, sending fiery waves of sensation coursing through her. It was, for the briefest second, overwhelming, and then it ebbed, and in its wake was the most pressing, driving need to be filled.

She groaned.

"I want to play first," he said, almost to himself, and then there was something pushing its way into her vagina. Not as big as Chance, not nearly, but plastic, hard, textured. And she already had a butt plug inside her.

He couldn't possibly...

He could. And he did.

Lena moaned loudly as he pushed the vibe into her, the feeling of being full now complete. He just kept pushing her, filling her, until she felt like a balloon ready to pop—she needed to come.

"Chance," she panted.

She was farther gone than she'd known; words wouldn't come.

He turned on the vibrator.

She was pretty sure she screamed. Yelled. Chance started to fuck her with it, moving it in and out of her with cruel slowness, twisting it so she felt the texture, raking it across her most sensitive nerves. It might have been the fastest orgasm in history. Fast, but not weak. He put his hand on her back, pressing her down into the pillows, just as she began to come, and not being able to move when the waves hit meant there was nowhere for the sensation to go but back inside her, folding in on itself, doubling and redoubling, until the resonance tore another scream from her throat.

She felt his hand on her butt, gripping her, as he pulled the vibe out of her. Immediately she missed it, missed the feeling of fullness, and he must have been able to tell, because he laughed.

"Now I'm going to take you," he said. "The way I've wanted you. Hard."

And he drove into her in one full stroke and she knew she cried out. Sobbed. Screamed. He was so perfect, so hot and thick, a little rough and very, very deep inside her. Chance fucked her like he said he would—hard, for his pleasure—and as soon as Lena thought of that she came again, not as quick to peak as the last time, but pulsing, squeezing, clenching around him for what seemed like forever.

He pulled out of her with a growl, and she knew he hadn't come. She was dazed, blind, and before she knew it he had uncuffed her wrists and flipped her over onto her back. She was dragged up the bed and her wrists were again quickly cuffed, this time above her head and attached to something on the headboard. Chance lifted her legs one at a time and attached cuffs just above the knee, so her legs were bent and spread.

Then something began pulling on her legs.

He'd attached the cuffs to leads somewhere above her head, maybe where her wrists were bound, and he was pulling on it so that her legs were pulled up, her knees by her head, and spread as far as they would go.

If she thought she was open and vulnerable before…

She felt pressure on the plug. Jesus. He was moving it around inside of her, reminding her of just what he was going to take. She wanted to move her hips, to move with him, to do *anything*, and still she couldn't. Her butt was lifted slightly off the bed, her arms and legs bound: she had no leverage, no movement.

She felt his breath on her thighs just moments before, but still she wasn't prepared for his tongue, inside her, probing. Lapping. He licked her from her entrance up to her clit, and then his tongue was working that swollen, intense bundle of nerves until she screamed again. She tried to writhe; all she had was sound, and she made a lot of it.

The contractions welled up from deeper inside her this time, like she'd been primed, her muscles warmed up, and now her entire body was in on it, pulsing and contracting and beating in time to a rhythm that quickly overtook her whole being.

She rattled the leads against the headboard.

"Goddamn, you are beautiful," she heard Chance say.

His hands were on her body then, soft and firm, rubbing down her trembling muscles, warming her damp skin. It seemed like a long time before she floated back into the present.

"How are your arms and legs?" he asked. "How's your circulation?"

Lena licked her lips. She could talk. Probably.

"I'm ok," she said.

"Good."

And then she felt it: more lube. He pushed the vibrator back into her vagina in one savage thrust, and Lena moaned. She was past anything, any thought, and fight, just ready to take whatever he would give her.

God, it felt good.

The plug moved slightly, and she realized he was pulling it out, and for just a second she was disappointed. Just a second. And then more cool lube, this time on her asshole, and Chance's strong, patient fingers, working it into her flesh, testing her.

She could feel it too — she was stretched.

Ready.

Oh God.

"Take a deep breath," he said.

His cock pressed against the tight ring and immediately she thought, *I can't.* Too much. Too big. With the vibe in her vagina she honestly didn't know if she could do this, but she wanted him, so, so badly. She gulped down air and tried to remember: breathe, bear down, relax.

He pushed into her with that same *pop*, that same *ohnoicant* followed by *more*. She wanted more. She could tell it was just the head of him, that he wasn't seated deeply inside. The pressure, the *need*, was almost unbearable.

"Chance," she croaked.

"Slow," he said.

More lube. He forced himself farther inside her, making her yelp and pull at her restraints. It felt too big, and yet she wanted more. She was stretched to the limit, so full she could burst, and all she wanted was for him to *move*.

"Almost," he said.

One last push, and Lena thought she would break. Her eyes were wide open behind her blindfold, her mouth open in a silent cry, overwhelmed by the stretch...

And then that faded, and she was left with every single muscle in her body primed and tight, ready for release. She needed him. Now.

"Chance…"

The blindfold came off. Lena blinked into the light, adjusting. Chance hovered over her, supported by his two strong arms on either side, his eyes…

"Look at me."

She locked her eyes with his and he started to move. Slowly. So, so slowly, his eyes never leaving hers. She didn't think to speak, wouldn't have known what to say if she had. She didn't need to. Everything she needed was right there in front of her.

He rocked her to another shattering orgasm.

Her memory was spotty for a time after that. She remembered that he carried her to the shower, after she was too weak to stand, and cleaned them both. She remembered him holding her, like he always did afterwards. She remembered thinking how lucky she was to fall asleep in those arms.

She tried to think of all these things when she woke up in the middle of the night, next to Chance, and felt the panic.

It wasn't the same as all those other times; it wasn't primarily defensive. It was raw. It was that, in the aftermath of all that, Lena didn't have the strength to lie to herself. And when all those defenses fell away, what she was left with was the bare truth that she loved him.

It was terrifying.

It was beautiful, and happy, and full of so much promise and risk, and it was terrifying. She tried it out in her head first: *I love him.*

Yup.

Still true. And she didn't have a panic attack — not quite.

She lay awake for hours trying to get up the strength to say it. Chance slept next to her on his side, one huge arm thrown over her body. Just his arm was heavy enough that she had to move it off of her chest so she could breathe. She cuddled into him, her face close to his, and watched him sleep.

Then she tried it.

"I love you, too," she whispered.

Her chest tightened, her lungs felt like they had a hole in them, but she tried to quell it, stop it before it could take root. It was an epic struggle taking place in her relatively tiny body, silent and immobile, weak and strong at the same time.

The one thought she couldn't kill, the one thing that kept returning to bring the dread and the panic back, was this: love wasn't enough. He said he loved her, but he hadn't had to deal with her too long. He hadn't had to deal with her freaking out the way she was now.

She hadn't even been able to say it back. None of it was fair. None of it was what he deserved.

Even worse? That slow, creeping feeling that she wasn't able to hold off any longer, the one telling her to run away and hide before she got hurt again—that need to flee wasn't fair to Chance, either.

Lena felt a tear run down the side of her face.

"I need to talk to Thea," she whispered.

chapter 24

Lena might have thought twice about knocking on Thea's door in the middle of the night if her lights weren't all on. That was unusual; Thea wasn't really a night owl.

It was only when Thea opened the door in a nightgown that Lena got worried.

"Thea, I'm sorry, I know it's the middle of the night, I just—"

"You know you're lucky I'm alone?" Thea said, not quite able to keep herself from smiling.

That shut Lena up.

"Wait, really?"

"I'm not *dead*, honey, I do still converse with other human beings from time to time. I'll tell you all about him in a second. Let me make some tea, and then you can tell me all about whatever's got you up in the middle of the night."

Just being in Thea's kitchen was a relief. Thea, who was the one person she had let her guard down around besides Chance, and that had taken years of hanging out with the woman daily. Lena always imagined that this was how comforting chats with your mother were supposed to go—a warm kitchen, tea, someone who knew you better than you knew yourself. She considered herself lucky that she got a second shot to have them, this time with someone who actually cared about her.

She had no idea what she'd do without Thea.

"What's wrong with your arm?" Lena asked.

Thea was favoring her left arm, holding it close to her body like she'd hurt it. Tea was marginally harder to make in that position.

"It's nothing," Thea said, shrugging. "Just been bothering me today. Part of getting older."

"You going to tell me about your boyfriend?"

Thea turned and scowled. "Don't make it sound like I'm thirteen. It's much more dignified than that."

Lena's jaw dropped.

"Ha!" Thea cackled. "Dignified. Yeah, I went down to the country club and snagged the fattest guy chomping down on a cigar I could find. Please, Lena."

"You are acting thirteen, FYI."

"My prerogative. Falling in love makes you dumb at any age."

Lena put down her tea, unable to keep herself from smiling. "In love?"

Thea put her nose up in the air and dunked a cookie into her tea. "Well, what do you think I've been doing while you've been off having some sexual adventure? Sitting at home?"

"Where did you find him? A casino? A strip club? An underground cockfight?"

Thea laughed again, and it made her look about ten years younger until she coughed slightly. She sipped her tea slowly, but Lena didn't miss the frown on her face. She didn't know what to make of it.

"The beach. He was painting the most hideous portraits, and when I realized he thought they were funny, I asked him out."

"Name?"

"John."

"Age?"

"Hush."

"Occupation?"

"World's most fabulous man. No, silly, he's retired. Used to be a stockbroker, now he has a houseboat."

"A houseboat! Are you guys going to go on cruises? Like up and down the coast?"

Thea narrowed her eyes over her teacup, and the effect was impressively menacing. Lena knew she'd been caught.

"You didn't come over here to talk about my love life or houseboats," Thea said. "Now you're just avoiding. Out with it, while I'm still young."

Lena looked down; she had destroyed her napkin, tearing it up into tiny little pieces. She hadn't touched her cookie. And she could feel the constriction building in her chest.

"You're lost your mind over Chance, haven't you?" Thea asked.

"How did you know?"

"Please. Look at you. I've never seen you so wrapped up in anything that you didn't call for weeks at a time. You look like you haven't slept in ages, and now you look miserable. Obviously it's love."

Lena grimaced. Yeah, Thea was more right than she knew. Love was the whole problem.

"He told me he loves me," she whispered.

Thea stared at her. Finally, she said, "Let me get my mourning dress."

"C'mon, be nice, Thea. I'm really messed up over this."

"Because you love him, too?"

Lena sighed. "Yes."

"You know, for most people this doesn't constitute a problem," Thea said.

"I know. That's why it *is* a problem. I'm too

much of a mess. I just...I can't do that to him."

Lena didn't want to see her friend's face as she said that, maybe because she was afraid it was as stupid as it sounded, maybe because she was just too raw already. That's how she missed what happened next.

~ * ~ * ~

Chance woke up and instantly knew Lena was gone.

It was the strangest thing—like a transfer of the kind of situational awareness he remembered from military missions. He just knew. Gone. His mind ran efficiently through all the possibilities. Most probably she was reverting to "irrevocably skittish" form; most likely destination: Thea's house. He would find her, they'd talk. It was time to stop coddling her.

He hunted down his phone and sent Thea a single text message: "She with you? She ok?"

~ * ~ * ~

Lena thought Thea was just prolonging the silence to make a point. To let the ridiculousness of Lena's fears sink in. Stubbornly, she rinsed her teacup out extra thoroughly, feeling dumber by the minute.

When she turned around, Thea was pale.

Short of breath. Clutching at her arm.

Funny how fear works. That moment seemed to last forever.

"Thea?" Lena asked. "Thea, what's happening?"

Thea shook her head. "I don't know," she said. "Can't breathe. My chest...tight..."

Thea wasn't even sitting upright now, just slumped over the table, like she didn't have the strength. Lena was petrified. She fumbled for a phone, sure one moment that this was an emergency, sure the next that Thea would recover in a second and make fun of her for panicking. The operator picked up and Lena felt such a rush of relief as she explained the situation, sure that the operator was going to tell her they'd send someone, but probably it was fine, Thea was going to be fine, everything—everything was fine.

"An ambulance is on the way. Do you have any aspirin in the house?"

Lena felt cold. Aspirin.

Thea was having a heart attack.

Chance must have been in the shower when the ambulance came, because he didn't hear the sirens. If he'd heard the sirens, he would have known right away. As it was, he came out in his towel and saw the lights, the red and blue lights, so weakly reflecting off the wall on the roof garden that he might have missed them.

He felt ice cold.

Walked out. Saw Lena's house. Thea's house. An ambulance, driving away, sirens blaring, lights flashing.

By the time he had his clothes on, there was a text waiting for him. Thea had had a heart attack. Lena was going to the hospital. No one was ok.

He found Lena in a waiting room looking like hell. Nobody looked good in hospital waiting rooms, and, as if to emphasize that point, every hospital he'd ever been in went for fluorescent lighting. So a woman who was already distraught and crying her eyes out had that to look forward to, too. He'd seen people get upset about the stupidest things in hospitals—you can't do anything about what's actually upsetting you, so you go mad over stupid shit.

Whatever. He was just glad to find her. She was beautiful to him, even when she was sobbing.

Neither of them said anything. She stood there, under buzzing, flickering lights, eyes red, cheeks wet, looking scared as hell, and he thought: *Ok, no talking.* He just walked up to her and wrapped her in his arms.

They stayed like that for a long, long time. Long enough for her shoulders to stop shaking, long enough for her to relax and then tense up all over again, clearly long enough for her to start thinking herself into a hole again.

He knew what she was going to say before she opened her mouth.

"I'm sorry, Chance," she said, hoarse from grief. "I can't handle this."

Normally Chance wasn't one to argue with people about what they did and didn't need, what they could and couldn't do. Wasn't his business. Only this time, it was. This time it was Lena. And she was wrong.

"Which thing, Lena?"

"Any of this. I can't handle losing…" She looked back in the direction of the emergency room and choked on her words.

"They haven't told you anything yet?"

Lena shook her head, mute. Chance held her face close to his.

"I'm not going anywhere," he said. He meant it.

But Lena just kept shaking her head, and he could see already the storm building inside her, that there were too many things going on at once, that a woman who was already scared had just been overloaded.

"No," she said. "Chance, I can't handle…oh God, I can't handle any of this."

"Doesn't change how I feel."

Tears welled up in her eyes again, and Chance could have kicked himself.

"No, that's just it. I can't afford to feel anything right now. I am too screwed up, Chance, I can't…"

"Shh…" he said, holding her again.

"I *can't*," she said again, but her arms held him tight.

"Somebody screwed you up good, huh?"

"No worse than any others. I got kicked out a lot, ended up on my own. It doesn't really matter," she said, pushing off his chest, "whether my mother was terrible, or people took advantage of me, or whatever. Plenty of people get over stuff like that, I know, I just…I can't. I'm not strong enough to get over it, and it's messed me up completely, and I just can't, *can't* do that to you, too. I can't lose Thea, and I can't… It won't work, Chance. It'll break me."

She broke away from him completely now, took a few steps back, as if to reinforce the space between them. The freaking gulf she was trying to put there. Chance wasn't fazed. He hurt for her, he hurt to see her in so much pain, but one thing had crystallized for him perfectly: it was a problem of faith, so to speak. All of it. She really didn't believe that the world would treat her right, she didn't believe in herself, and she was cutting herself off before she got hurt even worse.

It made a grim kind of sense. And it made

Chance suddenly understand exactly what it was that Lena did for him—she *believed in him*. Unquestioningly, in a way he'd never deserved. And it had made him better.

This woman who had no faith in herself at all, had put enough faith in him to make him a better man.

He knew what he had to do.

Chance waited while a man in scrubs carrying a clipboard came out to talk to her—he should have guessed Lena would be legally empowered for Thea. He bet it ran the other way, too, and the thought made him briefly happy, to know Lena had trusted someone. It made him even happier when he saw the relief on her face, when she smiled through tears.

"Good news?" he asked, gently.

She nodded, suddenly looking very tired. "She's going to be ok. Well, as ok as you can be after a heart attack. It wasn't a big one, but she's going to be here for a little while, and I have to go get her things, and…"

She looked back at Chance and met his eyes. The sadness in her eyes killed him.

"I am so sorry," she said.

He took her hand in his.

"Lena, sweetheart, I love you, but you're wrong," he said. "It will work, you do deserve it, you can afford it, and I'm going to prove it to you. You keep your phone. And you call me if   you   need   anything."

chapter 25

Lena woke with a start, her neck already cramping. Hospital chairs sucked. Why? Why, if you knew people were going to be sleeping in them, would you buy chairs that were so uncomfortable?

She rolled her neck and heard it crack sickeningly. She was going to be in terrible shape if this kept up.

"Morning, sleepyhead."

Lena's eyes shot open. "Thea?"

"The one and only."

Thea was trying to joke, but her voice was scratched and sore, and she had no color at all. Lena was torn—she was unbearably happy to see Thea up and talking and just being *Thea*, but it was the first time she'd ever seen Thea look...frail.

It was terrifying.

"How are you feeling?" Lena asked, moving to Thea's bed. It felt so good just to hold her friend's hand and feel Thea squeeze back.

"Better than I look, probably," Thea said. "They told me that's normal, and that you shouldn't be scared."

"You're lying, aren't you?"

"No, though I would if I needed to. Stop looking at me like you've seen a ghost."

Lena laughed, kissed Thea's hand, her forehead, her cheek. Her family was back.

"Sorry. I told you I was screwed up, remember?"

"Excuses, excuses. Oh no," Thea said, suddenly worried. "Have you told John?"

"Oh, shit," Lena said. She'd only just heard of the guy, but that wasn't an excuse, as Thea would say. She hadn't even thought of him. "No, but I can. I'll call him."

"Please," Thea said. "He's probably been calling me or been by the house. His number's on the fridge and in my phone. Do you have my phone?"

Lena checked her bag—she knew she had Thea's phone. "Crap. Battery's dead. It must have been searching for a signal, I didn't even think. I'll go back to the house and call him right away."

"Hold on one second," Thea said. She was too tired to sit up properly, and her voice sounded like she'd swallowed sand, but the woman could still deliver a Look like nobody's business. "You came to talk to me about Chance. What did you do about that?"

"Thea…"

"You're not using me as an excuse, are you?" Thea demanded.

Ouch. That…that hit close to home. What was Lena supposed to say?

"I wouldn't call it an excuse," Lena said carefully. "More like an illustration of a point I'd already made."

"Lena," Thea said sharply. "What did you do?"

Lena felt just as dumb as she had in the kitchen. Something about Thea's no-bullshit style and penetrating stare could make the most gifted debater wilt, and Lena wasn't entirely confident in the first place. In fact, she *knew* her decision, and her reasons for them, weren't entirely rational. But that didn't mean they were wrong. Emotions, people, hearts, and minds — they were rarely rational. That's what made them fun.

And what made them dangerous.

"I told him it wouldn't work," she confessed. "I told him I was too screwed up. And it's true, Thea, you know it is."

Thea gave an exasperated sigh and somehow managed to turn up the intensity on that stare.

"You are an idiot, you know that?"

"Yes?"

"Listen to me," Thea said, pointing a finger. That got Lena's attention. She couldn't remember Thea ever, ever pointing a finger at her. "You're afraid of getting your heart broken one day, so instead you're going to break two hearts today? You're afraid of losing happiness eventually, so you're just going to make sure you're never happy in the first place? Do you see how that makes no sense at all?"

Lena looked at the cold linoleum floors, the weight of Thea's logic proving too much. She was too tired.

"It's not supposed to make sense," she said finally. "It just is."

~ * ~ * ~

This had been easier than Chance thought it would be. Adra had gotten him an address, somewhere in the Hollywood Hills, and boom. Done. Now he was standing on the steps, waiting patiently for Roddy Nichols to get up and get over his hangover.

When the door opened, Chance didn't wait. He walked in, pressing a binder to Roddy's chest.

"Dalton? What the hell are you doing?" Roddy said. He looked like he needed sleep.

Sleep and possibly some detox.

"I'm going to make you some coffee," Chance said, calmly walking through the open house to a gorgeous glass-walled kitchen. "And you're going to read that for me, right now, and then you're going to tell me what you think of it. That's what we're doing."

Roddy followed him, waddling as fast as he could. "What? You can't just show up unannounced—"

"Obviously I can," Chance said, opening cupboards until he found a coffee grinder. This guy had a nice set up. "C'mon, Roddy, I'm a good guy to have in your debt. Besides, I'm not leaving until you do it, so it's not like you have a choice. You don't even have to like it. You just have to read it. You like it ground fine or coarse?"

Roddy slumped onto his breakfast bar in defeat, binder in hand. "Fine. But make me a Bloody Mary, too, will ya? Otherwise this is going to get a whole lot worse before it gets better, believe me."

~ * ~ * ~

Thea was just *not* going to let it go. And now that John was here—John, who was this ridiculous silver-haired dreamboat, all doting gestures and dirty jokes and a deep tan—he had ganged up on her, too.

"It's not just me," Lena tried to explain for the millionth time. "It's him. That's the point. I can't do this to him. I can't do it to myself. If you saw a disaster coming, wouldn't you try to avoid it?"

Thea harrumphed. "John, do me a favor? Get us some coffee?"

John smiled, his eyes crinkling in that distinguished way some men have. "I will give you some private time, yes. But you don't get coffee. Caffeine, remember?"

"Pseudoscience," Thea mumbled, but Lena saw her eyes as she followed John out. Yeah, she loved him. And he clearly loved her.

It was the major bright spot in Lena's life, at the moment.

"You are actually more of an idiot now than you were yesterday," Thea said.

"I can't, Thea," she said, quietly. "I can't do that to him."

"What? Give him what he wants? You dummy, I want to see you happy before I die, and apparently that could be sooner than I planned for. Listen, this is something you don't understand," Thea said, propping herself up on her pillows. "Me? I'm meant to be on my own most of the time. It's just how I'm built. And John *gets* that. He's the same way. We work together, we fit. But that is not how you're built, honey. That's why you keep trying with all kinds of guys who aren't right for you, even though you don't think you'll ever find love. Have you ever stopped to think about that? How strange that behavior is?"

Lena sat down, her butt protesting against the horrid hospital chair one last time. "Actually, no."

"Yeah, well, this time you've found him, and you're screwing it up. Look at me, Lena. You're just scared, but you need that boy. He gets that. Why don't you?"

~ * ~ * ~

Lola kept giggling. *Giggling.* To the point where Chance was starting to worry.

"What is wrong with you?" he asked her.

Immediately his cousin put on her game face. "Nothing. Honestly. I swear."

Chance stared at her. So that was a lie. But he didn't have time to figure out what the hell was going on with Lola at the moment. They had an appointment of sorts, and his plan had to work.

"Did Ford set you up?" he asked.

"I set me up," Lola said, looking down into her cleavage. "Roman would kill me if I let another man tape a microphone there, good cause or no. But Ford tested it. It works."

"Good. You remember the deal?"

"Yes, and it's delightfully ridiculous. I've never gotten to do spy versus spy stuff,

Chance, this is pretty awesome."

"This ain't a fun outing for your amusement," he said, glowering. "It's to help Lena."

Suddenly Lola fixed him with that lightning glare, and he knew he had nothing to worry about. "Chance, I am not going to allow this scumbag to get away with blackmailing you or extorting Volare, and I'm certainly not going to let him get away with hurting Lena. Let's go get this bastard on tape."

Chance smiled and pulled his car into the lot below Paul Cigna's apartment complex.

"We're already here," he said.

~ * ~ * ~

Lena rode the elevator up to Thea's floor feeling…well, she should have been feeling better. The first night of sleep in her own bed, a shower, fresh clothes. She should have been miles ahead of where she'd been yesterday.

Instead, though, there was the growing sense that things were profoundly wrong.

She tried to shake it off until she arrived at Thea's room to find it empty. She would have flipped out—she did flip out for about a second—but one of the nurses caught her.

"She's upstairs," the nurse said. "Moved to a private room."

A private room?

Upstairs?

Lena hadn't been aware that hospitals had different levels of comfort, but apparently this one did. She walked into Thea's new room to find her friend reclining on a pile of pillows, resplendent in her luxury, doing her best Gloria Swanson impression.

Lena laughed. "Seriously?"

"I only have one more night," Thea said regally. "It might as well be a good one."

"Ok, but how can you afford this?"

"My treat," a voice said from behind her.

The voice.

Chance.

Lena would have thought that, at such a profound moment, she'd have equally profound thoughts, something that fit the occasion. But no. What she thought was, *Thank God I washed my hair.* The next thing she thought was, *My God, look at him.* As always, he was effortlessly gorgeous, the sun from the big windows on the top floor shining on those eyes, that chin, that chest. He looked comfortable, thumbs in his front pockets, his jeans worn and relaxed, his shirt hanging flawlessly off his shoulders. But more than that he looked comfortable to *her*—he looked like home.

"Oh Jesus," she said.

Lena felt all the familiar signs: her stomach lurched, her chest tightened. She had no idea what she was going to do. What he was going to do.

"Don't mind me," Thea called from her bed of luxury. "Just pretend I'm not here."

"If you pretend to be asleep, I'll get you one of those little drinks with an umbrella in it," Chance said to Thea. His eyes held Lena's steadily. She couldn't have moved if she'd tried.

"Done," Thea called.

"Chance…" Lena tried.

"Quiet," he said. "I need you to listen."

Lena blinked. She obeyed, instinctively, and she was glad to, it made sense to her, and she was just so happy to have anything at all make sense—and at the same time, there was a softer edge to what he'd said. To the look he was giving her. To the way he came over and held her hands.

"There's some things I have to show you first," he said, getting his phone out of his back pocket. "It's pretty clear to me, Lena, that you still don't trust the world to treat you right. You don't think good things can happen for you. You don't believe in anyone, least of all yourself. Well, that is some bullshit. Watch."

His phone started to play a shaky video, something he'd evidently shot himself. An auteur Chance was not, but Lena recognized the man on camera immediately: Roddy Nichols. Roddy Nichols, looking miserable and hungover in his bathrobe. Reading from a binder—*her* binder. Her script.

"What—" she murmured.

"Wait for it," Chance said.

On screen, Roddy Nichols flipped to the last page in the binder, then flipped back to the beginning, then looked up at the camera in alarm.

"Where the hell's the end?" he demanded.

"Oh God," Lena said.

"How the hell does it end?" Roddy said, standing up.

Chance's voice could be heard off camera, saying, "So it's good, then?"

"What are you, slow? Of course it's good—it's amazing. I need to know how it fucking ends!"

Lena could actually *hear* Chance smile with what he said next. "I can get you in touch with the writer."

"You see that?" Chance said to her, happy as a puppy. "You see what he said? I told you!"

"Chance, what did you do?"

"I showed up at his house, made him coffee, and told him I wouldn't leave until he read it. And I told him I wanted an honest opinion."

Do not cry.

Do not cry.

Do not...

"What?" he asked her. "What's wrong?"

Lena shook her head, unable to deal with the unbearable sweetness of this man who she already knew was too good for her. "That's one of the nicest things anyone's ever done for me," she said.

"This?" Chance said, eyebrow up. "No way, that was nothing. Not a big deal. But I also got you something else," he said. "I'm not one hundred percent sure of the legalities, but Ford's fixing it. Upshot is, Lola and I got Paul Cigna on tape trying to extort me and you and whoever else he could get at. Dude is going to jail. The pictures are going into a shredder."

Lena stared at him.

"Or into the trash bin, whatever you do with digital files. But gone. Destroyed. No more. You never, ever have to worry about it, ever again," he said, and his earnestness killed her. He wasn't asking for anything. He just wanted her to know it was done.

"Thank you," she whispered.

Every single thing Chance did made her feel loved and broke her heart all at the same time. How could she ever live up to this? How could anyone?

"Chance," she said.

"I'm not done," he said. "Don't get all doom and despair on me until you hear me out."

Lena laughed. "I am a little like droopy dog at the moment. Stop making me laugh, it's not fair."

"I have never, ever played fair," he said, grinning. "Ok, now, for real, listen to me. Just be quiet. Here it comes."

He didn't have to tilt her head up this time to meet his eyes. She did it on her own. It was the least she could do, to meet this beautiful, loving, ridiculous man on his own terms.

"Ok," she said.

"I have an idea about what's holding you back, Lena. Let me roll with it. I believe in you, and I'm not wrong. You should believe in yourself, that good things can happen to you. I want to make that happen, I will work my ass off to make that happen, but I know why you're resistant."

"I—"

"What did I say?" he said, cocking his head.

She shut up.

"But don't pretend this makes sense, Lena, this is just about you being scared. You almost lost Thea, and that reminded you how much you suck at needing people."

Lena opened her mouth to object, but hesitated. She couldn't even argue the point anymore. He was one hundred percent correct. She was actually waiting for Thea's chorus of agreement, and was kind of relieved to realize she probably couldn't hear it.

"Did you conspire with Thea?" she asked him.

"What? No. Why?"

"Sorry."

"Don't change the subject," he growled, and hooked his finger into the waist of her jeans, pulling her in close. "I know you love me, Lena, and I know why you don't trust that. Why you don't trust the world to work out, or people to be there for you. I think you will trust me to be there, eventually. I'll do everything I can to make sure you can believe in me, in time. But right now, you need to know that *I need you*."

Those last three words hit Lena like a glass of ice water: *I need you*. In all her pining, in all her tortured thinking, her rationalizations, her internal debates about what to do about Chance, she had never once considered the possibility that he needed her. She'd accepted that he loved her, she'd accepted that she loved him, even that she needed him, but the stumbling block was, once she got over that, how she would inevitably mess it up. How her profound inability to trust in anyone or anything except maybe after years and years would test any man to the limit, how he would get tired of her, tired of dealing with it, tired of all of it, and it would eventually destroy both of their lives.

She didn't know what to do with that. He needed her?

"Lena, look at me," Chance said. "I told you about all that shit in my past, all the times I've been violent, all the times I've been scared of what I was. Look at this."

He held up his phone again. There was a picture of Richie Kerns. Lena jumped, and Chance swiped to the next picture: Paul Cigna. Both of them were smiling.

"What? Why would you show me that?" she asked.

"Look again," he said. "Anything you notice? Like how both men are in perfect health?"

It wasn't something you'd notice unless someone pointed it out, but yes, both of them appeared to be in perfect health, if smiling a little strangely. Almost…strained.

"I didn't touch them, even when provoked," Chance said. "And Cigna tried to provoke me when I went over there the last time, believe me, because he wanted the lawsuit. He actually came after me. But because of you…it's because you make me better. Because you make it possible for me to be a better man."

Lena was stunned. She had no inkling, no understanding.

"Chance, I don't—"

"Not done, sweetheart," he said, putting one finger on her lips. "You don't fix me, I'm not saying that. But you make me want to be better, and you make it easier. I don't know if that's good, but I do know I don't give a shit anymore if it's not. It just *is*, and there's nothing anybody can do about it. I love you now, I'll love you for fucking ever. You've made me a better man, whether you like it or not, and I fucking *need* you. Don't take that away from me because you're afraid to need me, too."

Lena had no words. She was overcome. She was felled. She was utterly, utterly decimated by this man. By the idea that the strongest man she'd ever known, the one who'd stood up for her, who'd stood by her, who'd put so much work into helping her, just because she'd asked — that he might need her.

"Chance, I don't know what to say," she said.

"Say you'll give this a shot. A real shot. I believe in you more than anything else on this planet. I know you're brilliant, and kind, even when you try to be a smart ass, and you're right for me, and you're the best woman I know, and if you can't believe that yet, I will for the both of us, until you can catch up."

Then he leaned down to whisper in her ear. "This is the one and only time I'm ever going to beg you for anything, sweetheart," he said. "But you better believe you're gonna pay for it later."

Lena tucked her head into the hollow of his neck to hide her smile and her tears, and then on impulse kissed him there. When she pulled back to look into those eyes once more, they were shining.

"Yes," she said.

From behind her came a familiar voice. "Hallelujah!" Thea said.

epilogue

Lena took a big lungful of ocean air and tried not to be worried for Thea. This was, after all, a joyous kind of thing, right? An alternative wedding, of sorts? No, definitely a happy occasion.

But Lena was still Lena, and her adopted family was about to go on a month long sailing trip down the coast with her new, "technical" husband, as Thea put it. So she was worried.

John had insisted that they get legally married, after Thea got out of the hospital, and he'd made too many rational arguments, all of which Lena happened to agree with—it was important for John to be able to get into the hospital, for example, and it would help Thea to be on his crazy amazing insurance. Also, if she were being honest, Lena was totally happy to turn the tables and gang up on Thea about her man. They had made it a marriage of their own style, though—Thea valued her independence too much, and so did John. She kept her house, he kept his houseboat. This trip was going to be interesting.

Which was how most of Volare L.A. was gathered at Marina del Ray to see the beaming, glowing, ridiculously happy couple off. It served as a kind of ad hoc wedding celebration, reception, and general excuse to make Thea uncomfortable. Lena did love that.

And she also loved how quickly Volare had embraced Thea. She was vaguely concerned, for a while, that she'd have to keep these parts of her life separate, but the second she'd confessed that concern to Adra, Thea had been brought into the fold. Not the fold that consisted of subs being to tied to a St. Andrew's Cross on Friday nights kind of fold—thankfully, for Lena—but the fold that included barbecues and private concerts and, apparently, going away parties at Marina del Ray.

And of course, there was Chance. Always Chance. The life of the party wherever he went, the guy who made sure everyone was ok, her Chance. It still made Lena smile to think that he was hers. *Hers.* Right now she was watching him hold court at the other end of the covered outdoor area adjacent to the boathouse, apparently trying to learn how to do a fire-eating trick, with Thea clapping along happily.

Actually, on second thought, maybe she *wouldn't* watch that. If she looked over again in a second and he was still putting fire anywhere near that beautiful face, she'd have something to say about it. It would just be a bonus if she got disciplined for it later.

"Hey you," Adra said, showing up by Lena's side with a glass of sparkling wine. Adra was another invaluable addition to Lena's life—she'd proved to be a true friend, taking Lena's script and going to freaking battle for it. She'd actually managed to sell it, and when Adra made the announcement, you could have knocked Lena over with a feather. Which was just as well, because Chance had picked her up and refused to put her down for the rest of the night.

"Hey!" Lena smiled. "Have you seen Lola? I got her some Ghirardelli chocolates, assuming she's still into chocolate, and not, like…"

"Pickles? Mayo on onions? Some other unholy combination?" Adra laughed. "Yeah, she's over there, behind Chance and his crowd, but good luck getting anywhere near her without a security pass. Roman is ridiculous."

Roman's overprotectiveness had been the highlight of the couple's visit. Thea had invited them personally, after she'd found out how much Lola had helped out with

Lena's...difficulties...accepting Chance, and Lola was definitely showing, and Roman had the curious look of a man determined to protect his woman at all costs who was also completely and utterly dazed. Lena would think he was all lost in thought, this dreamy look on his face while he wondered about his unborn child, and then Lola would so much as wince at some back pain and the man would jump into action.

It had almost gotten to the point where it was fun to mess with him. Almost. Chance had an eagle eye, and Lena wasn't going to cross from funishment into punishment—too often, at least.

"Hey, who's that?" Lena asked.

She had spotted a woman wearing what looked like a very restrictive, business-y sort of blouse, a staid, conservative skirt, and terribly uncomfortable shoes, all of which kind of made her stand out among the Volare L.A. crowd. She also had a notebook, something that set off alarm bells for Lena. She still wasn't a fan of the press, though she was working on it.

But this particularly woman, who really was very attractive under all that fuss, was being given a hard time by what looked like college kids attached to another boat down the dock. Lena frowned.

"And what the hell are they doing to her?"

Adra followed her gaze and muttered, "Damn. That's the writer I hired for Declan."

"The what now?"

Adra smiled. Her and Ford had been busily trying to help Declan Donovan rehabilitate his image after what was collectively referred to as the "Philadelphia Incident." The press coverage had been awful, and it had only cemented Declan's reputation as a sex god womanizing boozehound. He'd gone through rehab and come out sober, but lost some of his bandmates as a result—the man was definitely in transition. And there was clearly something bigger underlying his fling with self destruction.

But he'd been one of the nicest guys Lena had encountered, ever, totally down to earth, and apparently oblivious to the effect he had on most women. Volare seemed like a good place for him, but a writer?

"We commissioned her to write a biography," Adra said, eyes narrowing as the college kids grew more bold. In fact, they looked kind of drunk. "Or memoir, whatever. Something to get Declan's story out there. Her writing is superb, but I didn't think she'd be so…"

"Fusty?"

"Formal, maybe? I mean, it's important that she and Declan get along."

Lena and Adra watched as the woman

deftly handled the drunken idiots on her way to their group. Still, there was a limit to what any single woman could do in that situation.

"We better go help her," Lena said.

Both women girded themselves to go deal with some drunk boys intent on harassing any female within shouting distance, knowing Ford and Chance would probably be at their sides in about two seconds flat—especially Ford, who Adra claimed she wasn't at all interested in, to everyone's amusement—when Declan crossed their paths, making a beeline for the writer in question.

"Oh, boy," Adra said under her breath. "I can't tell if this is really good, or really bad."

"It's definitely really something," Lena agreed.

Declan had descended on the drunk regatta-styled fratboys like a nightmare. Really, any of the Volare members would have done the same, but no one else would have brought quite the same tattooed, hugely muscled rock god badassness to the venture. The looks on the drunk boys' faces were absolutely priceless—they didn't know whether to apologize or ask for an autograph.

Instead they just scattered.

And yet, the look the writer gave Declan was...pissed off? Flustered? And yet totally checking Declan out?

"Whaaaat is going on there," Adra

whispered.

Lena smiled. It was sort of nice to see something like this from her perspective, having finally yielded to Chance, and finding out that it made her happier than she'd ever been. "I take it they have to spend some time together?" she asked Adra.

"Yup."

"So this is going to be fun?"

"That, or a disaster. One of the two."

"Like most things," Lena smiled.

Suddenly she felt two strong arms sliding around her waist from behind, and Chance's broad chest at her back. Lena's face erupted into huge smile, like it always did, and she relaxed into him.

"What are you two ladies planning?" he asked. Warm gravel again. Lena bit her lip.

"Global takeover," Lena said.

"We've decided to become super villains," Adra added.

Lena felt Chance nuzzle her hair. She was having all sorts of responses that weren't remotely appropriate for a public marina.

"Adra, I think Ford might need your help with whatever's going on over there," Chance said.

Adra looked at Chance, looked at Ford talking to Declan and the writer, then looked at Lena. It was apparent that Ford didn't need any help at all. Adra just smiled.

"Oh, of course," she said, winking at Lena. "I'll talk to you later?"

"Always," Lena said. She turned in Chance's arms to face him, wrapping her arms around his neck.

"Why'd you scare Adra off?" she said. But she was already getting heated, just touching him. Sometimes she wondered if this attraction would ever wear off, but somehow she knew it wouldn't—it wasn't normal, what they had, and she loved it.

And those *eyes*.

"Did you say goodbye to Thea?" he asked.

"I did not say goodbye," Lena said. "I said see you soon."

"Good. I have something to show you."

Lena bounced on her toes. "Did you find a house?"

Thea had insisted that Lena keep her apartment, and Lena had been grateful for the gesture, something that helped her with her initial anxieties. But she hadn't spent one night there. And Chance, meanwhile, had been looking for a house he deemed worthy.

Chance grinned, and his hands slipped down to her hips, his fingers resting lightly on her butt in a way that he knew drove her wild.

"I did. A few weeks ago. But now it's ready," he said. "One room in particular is ready."

Lena's heart fluttered. "One room?"

"There's a bench that needs breaking in," Chance said. "Immediately. Get your ass in the car."

Lena inhaled, wondering once again at how lucky she was. Then she jumped up, kissed her man, fuzzed his head, and said, "Thank you, sir."

THE END

A note from the author...

Hi! Thank you so much for reading *Taken by Chance*. I hope you enjoyed Chance and Lena's story, and that it brought you a bit of happiness. If you liked it, I hope you'll share it with friends you think might like it, too.

And I'd love to hear your thoughts on *Taken by Chance*! You can connect with me on Facebook or email me at chloecoxwrites@gmail.com, or leave a review on Amazon or on Goodreads. I sincerely appreciate every review — I think they help other readers out, and I learn something with every review, too.

'Till the next book!

Chloe

CPSIA information can be obtained at www.ICGtesting.com
Printed in the USA
LVOW06s1820130813

347707LV00001B/20/P